RUNAWAY

1961: In her second year as a probationary WPC at Stony End Station, Bobbie Blandford is tasked with investigating a murder that may have ties to the tragic deaths of two women before the war. Then a secret emerges from Doctor Leo Stanhope's past that brings a halt to their budding romance. Hurt and confused, Bobbie goes on secondment to Scarborough, where young policeman Steve Brown promises to help her find the answers to the murders — and her romantic woes . . .

Books by Sally Quilford
in the Linford Romance Library:

SALLY QUILFORD

RUNAWAY

Complete and Unabridged

LINFORD
Leicester

First published in Great Britain

First Linford Edition
published 2016

A catalogue record for this book is available
from the British Library.

ISBN 978–1–4448–2697–5

Published by
F. A. Thorpe (Publishing)
Anstey, Leicestershire

Set by Words & Graphics Ltd.
Anstey, Leicestershire
Printed and bound in Great Britain by
T. J. International Ltd., Padstow, Cornwall

This book is printed on acid-free paper

1

It was early spring, and there was still a nip of frost in the early morning air while I marched at the front of the line of police officers, with two female officers from other stations flanking me. It was a proud moment for me as a probationary WPC. I was dating Doctor Leo Stanhope, the best-looking man in Britain. I had a great friend in my landlady, Doctor Annabel North. And I had survived my first year of probation at Stony End police station. I had also found out some sad truths about my early life, but on this day, with wintry rays of sunshine lighting up the town of Stony End, I had come to terms with it.

Townspeople lined the route, waving flags. I forget what we were celebrating. It seems to me that when I was younger life was full of such parades, and there seemed to be one every week, either for religious or historical reasons, or just because we all liked an excuse for a street party or a picnic in the park. Most of those customs have fallen into disuse, but at the time it brought us all together. I can still see the packed lunches handed out to children, which contained a cheese sandwich, orange juice, a custard cream and an apple. There were no warnings about allergies. Children basically got what they were given and somehow they survived the experience.

A police officer is always on duty, even when leading a civic parade. So when the cry 'Stop, thief!' echoed in the brisk morning air, I broke ranks and ran in the direction of the shout, vaguely registering the laughter of the crowd and the sharp 'Get back in line, Blandford' of Sergeant Jack Simmonds, who marched behind me.

It was Bert Palmer, the butcher. 'Little beggar stole my sausages,' he gasped. He had only run a few feet, but full to the brim of his own produce,

Bert was not a great sportsman. 'Went in that direction.' He pointed towards the park, where a band was playing selections from *West Side Story*. So it was to a sprightly brass band version of *America* that I chased down the perpetrator.

'Stop! Police!' I called, almost slipping on a sausage which the thief had dropped along the pathway. 'Come back here!' I blew my whistle, thinking it might get his attention. 'Stop him!' I cried to several passers-by, but they just ignored me or laughed. How on earth was I meant to keep the peace if the public did not help me?

Finally I had him cornered near the fence at the top of the park. He was a lean and hungry-looking creature, with a mop of dark hair around his face, and it occurred to me that he needed the sausages much more than Bert did.

'Where did you come from, hey?' I asked. 'I've never seen you around here before, have I?' He looked a bit familiar, but I could not place where I had seen him. 'Come on,' I said, 'hand them over and I'll get you a decent meal.' He answered by swallowing the lot in one go. 'Ugh . . . ' I mean, I like sausages as much as the next person and I've even been known to eat a raw sausage (a delicacy that today's youth do not quite understand), but six at once?

The thief sat down. 'Come on,' I said again, approaching him gingerly.

'You'll need this,' said a familiar voice behind me. It was tinged with amusement. 'Make sure the judge throws the book at him. Rotten dirty thief.' My heart flipped and my spine tingled.

'Leo,' I said, grinning from ear to ear. 'Hello.'

'Hello, Bobbie.' He seemed more reserved than usual. Had I embarrassed him with my dash from the line? Leo knew me well enough to know I did not always do the right thing, though if I did the wrong thing it was usually for the right reasons.

He handed me a collar and lead. 'I

got it from the pet shop when I saw you running past,' he said, answering the question I was just about to ask. 'That's Dottie Riley's dog, Elvis, isn't it?'

★ ★ ★

It was nineteen sixty-one, and John F. Kennedy had become president of the United States, bringing a glamour to politics. Britain, with its crusty old prime ministers like Harold McMillan, could not begin to compete. Kennedy's administration was often likened to Camelot, and he seemed to have all the attributes of the once and future King Arthur. We were all hopelessly in love with him, having no idea at the time that the king we adored was completely naked — usually with Marilyn Monroe.

In that year *The Avengers* had just started on television, and Annabel and I were avid fans. She was watching it when I returned home with Elvis that evening. 'Can he stay?' I asked. 'Dottie Riley has gone off somewhere and left

5

him.' Dottie Riley was the owner of the local chip shop, and had been a good friend of my mother's in the years before the war.

'Really? That's not like her.'

'No, I know. Her sister reported her missing last week, but poor Elvis was forgotten about. The sister thought Dottie had taken him with her.'

'Can't the sister take him?'

'She says not. He's got nowhere else to go, Annabel.'

'What sort of dog is he, anyway?' We both looked at the black fluffy mutt at my feet. He had the most beautiful black eyes, and was looking much happier since I had nipped to the shop and got him a tin of dog food.

'A bit of everything, I think. Dottie got him from the RSPCA last year. It looks like he's been living rough for a while. Just until we find him a home, Annabel. Please. No one else at the station will take him.'

Annabel sighed and smiled. 'Very well. He can stay for a while. But he sleeps in your room and any mess, you clean it up.'

'Yes, Mother,' I said, grimacing.

She laughed. 'I did sound a bit stuffy, didn't I?'

'Yes, but . . . '

'But what?'

'I've got a date with Leo and I promised I wouldn't let him down again. He says he has something important to say.'

'A proposal?' Annabel sat up, giving me her full attention. 'It's about blinking time!'

'I don't know, and I won't unless I can go.'

Annabel stood up and took the lead from my hand. 'Come on, Elvis,' she said. 'It looks like I'm dog-sitting.'

'You're an angel.'

'I know. You owe me big time, Bobbie Blandford! I want a full report of the proposal. Does he get down on one knee? Does he produce a diamond the size of a football? Does he pay a man to play the violin?'

'I don't think that's Leo's style.'

'I don't know about that. He's changed since he met you. He even speaks to me nowadays.' Leo was a general practitioner, and Annabel was a junior doctor at the hospital, so their paths often crossed.

I grinned. 'Yes, he's changed, hasn't he? I think Joe Garland has helped.' Joe Garland was Leo's fifteen-year-old half-brother. Since Joe's mother had been imprisoned, Leo had been taking care of him.

'Joe had nothing to do with it. It's you, darling. Every time Leo sees you, his whole face lights up.'

With that happy thought I went to get ready for my date. I could hear Annabel downstairs talking to Elvis, giving him the ground rules. 'No sitting on the sofa,' she said. 'And no weeing on the rug. Oh, and absolutely no chewing my best shoes.'

Stony End was a market town in Derbyshire, full of the sort of stone-built cottages for which people pay a fortune nowadays just to live in a couple of weekends a year. Back then they were mainly workers' and artisans' cottages. The town boasted one pub, one chip shop, a newsagent's, a Woolworth's, a modern (for the time) supermarket, a church — St Jude's — and the obligatory butcher, baker and candlestick-maker. Though I don't think we actually had a candlestick-maker. There was a cobbler's shop that had a creepy marionette in the window in the shape of an old man. He bobbed up and down, knocking a rather vicious-looking nail into a pair of shoes. At Christmas the marionette wore a Santa suit. Rather than making him seem friendlier, it only added to his demonic air. If I were a child, I'd have run a mile from such a Father Christmas. As an adult, he still gave me the creeps.

Leo and I met at the Cunning Woman pub, as was our custom. Then we would choose somewhere else to go, either the pictures or somewhere to eat.

The Cunning Woman was a Tudor-style building in Stony End town centre with dark oak furnishings. The faces inside were always the same. There was something comforting about that, as there was with the customs and practices leading to street parties. It suggested continuity.

'How are you, WPC Blandford?' asked Brian Lancaster. He was the new owner, a jovial man of about fifty-five, but still very handsome, though his handlebar moustache did nothing for me personally. It set him apart from my generation. Nevertheless, he had set quite a few middle-aged female hearts fluttering in Stony End. It didn't hurt that he walked with a limp, due to shrapnel in his leg from his part in the Battle of Britain. Everyone loved a brave ex-serviceman and I suspected that Mr Lancaster lapped up their adoration.

'I'm fine, thank you, Mr Lancaster. I don't suppose you've seen Dottie Riley, have you? I have her dog, and . . . '

He stroked his moustache. 'Dottie? Is that the lady from the chip shop?'

'Yes, that's right. She seems to have gone off somewhere, and it's odd, her leaving her dog. And the chippy, for that matter. It's not like her.'

'Maybe I'll sell a few more pies now,' Brian said with a disarming grin. I thought he seemed a little unsympathetic, but reminded myself that he did not know Dottie Riley.

When I sat down Leo seemed nervous. Someone had put 'Will you Love me Tomorrow?' on the jukebox, and for some reason it made me nervous. Could he really be about to propose? Although we had known each other over a year, and had been through a lot together, we had not been dating that long.

I looked at his handsome face, taking in all the features. It was true that he had seemed happier lately. When I first met him the year before he had resembled an angry young man from a kitchen sink drama, like Richard Burton, despite

11

him being more a lord-of-the-manor type. That worried me a little. He could not possibly propose to me. True, my dad had been a policeman, and my mum was a policewoman before they married, but we were from a working-class background. It's hard to believe but in nineteen sixty-one, class still mattered. Only the year before, the obscenity trial over *Lady Chatterley's Lover* had led to the chief prosecutor asking if it was the sort of novel one would want their wives or servants to read. Some of the better-off members of society, even in a small place like Stony End, still had maids, gardeners and housekeepers. The feudal system had not quite died out.

'Well . . . ' I said after taking a sip from my Babycham. When I first started seeing Leo I had drunk gin and tonic in an attempt to seem more mature. I had become comfortable enough with him not to care anymore, but that night I wondered if I should have gone for the more sophisticated drink again. 'What did you want to talk to me about?'

He took a deep breath. 'You know how I feel about you, Bobbie. Don't you?'

'I . . . er . . . ' Something in his tone bothered me. 'I guess you must like me a bit, since we spend so much time together.'

'A bit . . . ?' He laughed incredulously.

'What is it, Leo? If it's over, just say so.' I was becoming panicked. 'We've had a nice time together, haven't we? But if you don't want to see me anymore, there won't be any recriminations or . . . or . . . ' I struggled to find the right words. 'I shan't hold it against you.'

'So you wouldn't be that bothered then?'

'Well, yes of course . . . ' That song was still playing in the background, and I wondered then if Leo had been the one to put it on, even though I was the one who desperately needed to know if Leo loved me, not just tomorrow, but at all. I liked to think of myself as a modern woman, but I was not that progressive. 'What I mean is, I'd never hold you back if you preferred to be somewhere else. Or with someone else.' This conversation was not going the way I expected. I doubted very much there was a diamond the size of a football, or a violin-player hiding in a back room waiting for his moment to play a romantic melody. I did notice that the door to the pub opened, but my mind was fixed on Leo.

'There is no one else, Bobbie. Oh . . . you're so hard to talk to some-times.'

'Am I? It's a wonder you spend any time with me then,' I snapped.

'I don't mean that. I mean . . . you never show your feelings. Well you do show your feelings. When there's a lost dog, or a runaway child. But you don't show your feelings to me. About me.'

I wanted to explain to him that I had been waiting for him to say he loved me. It was not the done thing for me to say it first. Girls can be more forward nowadays, but back then in the sixties some of the old values still held. This included the rule that the man had to be the one to do all the chasing.

'It doesn't mean the feelings aren't there,' I said. It was as close as I could come to telling the truth. Oh I daresay you want to bang our heads together, but I could not break away from the things I had been taught. Why could he not just say he loved me? That would make it so much easier.

'So we can go away for the weekend then? To London.'

'London? For the weekend?'

'That's what I wanted to ask you. To go away with me for the weekend.'

'Oh. Yes, why not?' It was not quite the proposal I had expected.

'Good. I'm glad we sorted that out.'

I took a sip of my Babycham and really did wish it was a gin and tonic, or something stronger still. Given the problems that Leo and I had experienced, I could not really expect a grand proposal. Because of those problems I

15

had held back on the passion, and I suppose he had the impression that I was not very romantic. Really I wanted him to be Gregory Peck, James Stewart and Richard Burton all rolled into one, treating me like Lana Turner, Elizabeth Taylor and Vivien Leigh. I wanted to be swept off my feet and carried up a grand staircase to consummate our love. But what else could I expect from the local doctor in a Derbyshire village? Derbyshire men were not known for their affectionate outbursts.

'Shall we go to the pictures?' he asked.

'Do you know what?' I said, rubbing my temples. 'I've got a splitting headache, so I might just call it a night.'

'I'll walk you back.'

We went back to the cottage in silence, constricted by this big thing that was happening between us. I had agreed to spend the weekend with him, which was a huge step in our relationship. So why did my heart ache so much?

I loved Leo. I still love Leo. That

feeling has never gone away. I knew without a doubt he was the man I wanted to marry. I just was not that sure I was the girl he would ever want to marry. Maybe it would ruin things if we went away together. What was that awful idiom? Why buy the cow when you can get the milk for free? So why on earth had I agreed? If the truth be known, I wanted him to think me sophisticated and in touch with the modern world. But inside I was just as quaint and old-fashioned as Brian Lancaster at the pub.

'Good night,' I said when I got to the cottage gate. There was a faint light coming from the sitting-room window.

Leo pulled me to him and I felt that old familiar longing as his lips found mine. His arms tightened around me, and for a moment I was lost in the passion for which I longed. He pulled away slowly. 'We'll have a great time, Bobbie. I promise.'

'Yes,' I said, but could not be as sure about it as him.

I went inside to find Annabel asleep on the sofa. She was half-sitting up, with Elvis lying next to her, his head on her lap. One of her shoes was in his mouth. She stirred on hearing me enter the room.

'He's asked me to go away with him for a dirty weekend,' I said.

'Congratulations, sweetie,' Annabel muttered sleepily, giving Elvis a celebratory pat on the head.

I burst into tears.

2

When Annabel woke up enough to hear the story properly, she was as disappointed as me. We sat in front of the fire, eating Spam sandwiches. Some people lose their appetite when they're upset. Unfortunately I'm not one of them. Elvis, who had already decided he was staying with us forever, even if we had not made up our minds, shared the leftovers.

'So no flowers or violins?'

'Not even a ring. Just a vague proposal to go to some crummy hotel in London for a weekend of illicit passion.'

'And you said yes?'

I nodded miserably.

'Hmm, we're hardly setting Stony End alight here, are we?'

'Life's not like the films though, is it?' I asked rhetorically. 'I mean, we can't expect to be swept off our feet. Me and

Leo are all right. We're comfortable together.'

'Ye gads,' said Annabel. 'Come Christmas you'll be wearing matching reindeer sweaters.'

'I need your help, Annabel. You're my best friend. Please say you'll talk me through how to behave. You know about this stuff.'

'Why, because I'm a trollop?' Annabel was joking.

'No, of course not! Oh, you're more sophisticated than I am. You know that.'

'I know, sweetie. But the main thing to remember is that if you don't want to go through with . . . ' She hesitated. ' . . . with it, you don't have to. You're allowed to say no at any time.'

I nodded, full of relief. That was comforting to know. 'Will you help me choose something nice to wear? My fashion sense is rubbish.'

'And yet you always look gorgeous.'

'Oh you silver-tongued charmer, you.' I tried to laugh, but instead another tear fell from my cheek. Annabel put her arms around me.

'It will be fine,' she soothed. 'I promise you. I know that Leo loves you and that you love him.'

'He's never said it.'

'Have you?'

'Of course not! How can I if he doesn't?'

Annabel sighed. She was a little more progressive than I was. When she saw a man she wanted, nothing held her back. I put it down to her being the daughter of a duke. She did not suffer from the same lower-class morality as me. I do not mean that she was more sexually experienced. Only more self-assured.

'Honestly, Bobbie. I really could bang your heads together!'

News travels fast in Stony End, and someone had obviously overheard me and Leo talking in the pub. The next day, when I was on duty at the station, people kept coming in on some pretext. The men's eyes glittered lasciviously whilst the women, usually in groups of two or three, harrumphed amongst themselves about falling moral standards.

Even Mrs Higgins turned up. She was dressed in a purple raincoat with bright yellow wellington boots. 'Those commies are sniffing around again,' she said, putting an old tin down on the counter. 'I won't be surprised if they drop the atom bomb on us before the year is out.'

Martha Higgins was a strange woman, with an even stranger attitude to the truth. Yet in many ways she was the most truthful person I knew. Her lips might lie, but her heart was honest. 'I thought I'd come and warn you,' she said. 'People talk a lot of rubbish around here, yet there's a lot goes on behind closed doors that none of them would want us to know about. Two young, unattached people enjoying themselves should not be cause for idle gossip. I thought you'd like some of my coconut sponge for your tea break. It'll take away the bitter taste of vicious tongues.' Mrs Higgins and I had shared quite a few cakes since we had met just over a year before. I often stopped by her caravan for a cup of tea, and either I took a cake or she had baked one.

'Thank you,' I said, trying not to cry. 'That's really kind. My colleagues will enjoy it too.'

'Remember when I read your tea leaves and told you that you'd met the man of your dreams?' she asked.

'Yes, it was the first day I moved to Stony End.' And not long after she had seen me talking to Leo Stanhope. 'Then you warned me against him.'

'Well, he was suspected of murder.'

'Mrs Higgins, we established that Leo . . . Doctor Stanhope was not a murderer.' I had thought Leo murdered my father, but thankfully that turned out not to be the case.

'It wouldn't be the first time in Stony End that a woman lost her heart to a charming man then paid the price with her life.'

'When was the last time?'

'It was in the late nineteen-thirties. Just as war broke out. In fact that's what I've really come to talk about. My sister, Ruth.'

'I'm sorry, Mrs Higgins,' I said, not really wanting to get dragged into one of her reminiscences. Especially if it was also another fantasy. 'I had no idea about your sister. But Leo was only a child then. I don't think he was murdering women, let alone having affairs with them.' Yet I had once believed him capable of killing my father and he had been little more than a child then.

'No, I'm not saying Stanhope did it. Two of them there were both found dead. One was found in the B and B in town, before it became the youth hostel. They found my sister in a room at that big hotel that used to be a stately home, out on the Stockport road. The Ladykiller they called him. I bet the files are down there in that cellar of yours.'

I realised then that the coconut cake was not to show approval of my life choices, but to bribe me into reopening the case. Since I had come to Stony End I had taken over the cold case files, which were kept in the cellar at the police station, and in my spare time I liked to reinvestigate them. It was how I had found my father's true killer and cleared Leo's name.

For the most part the cold cases were minor offences, like a recent one I had looked into about the theft of District Nurse Elsie Atkins's bicycle during the blackout. Elsie was now nearly eighty years old and living in a nursing home in Little Stony. It reminded me that I had promised to go and see her.

'What were the women's names?' I asked Mrs Higgins now, hating myself for rising to the bait. Realising I had been callous, I added, 'Sorry, I mean what was your sister's name?'

'Ruth Yates, that was my sister, and Betty Norris.'

'Norris? As in PC Alf Norris?' Alf Norris was my friend and mentor at the station. Still a constable in his fifties, he epitomised what old-time policing used to be, with a kind but firm word for any perpetrators.

'Oh yes, she was his cousin. I'd forgotten about that.'

'I don't know, Mrs Higgins. I know from personal experience how hurtful it can be to dig up the past. It might cause you more pain and Alf may not like it.'

'Alf won't like what?'

The man himself walked into the station. I faltered, but tact was not something from which Mrs Higgins suffered. 'You won't like her looking into the murder of your cousin, Betty and my sister, Ruth.'

'Ah . . . well, maybe a fresh pair of eyes will bring something new to it, eh? Besides, Bobbie is good at these things, and it'll cheer her up. She's been looking sad all morning.'

It was just like Alf to think of me before himself. 'Alf, I'm not sure I like you thinking that looking into your cousin's death would cheer me up.'

'It's a long time ago lass, and

26

. . . well, this will sound callous, and I don't mean it to be, but me and Betty weren't that close. She was . . . well her life was a bit different to mine. Not that I'm not sorry for what happened to her.'

'Yes, Pearl is the one you really want to ask about Betty,' said Mrs Higgins.

Pearl was a local prostitute, so the mention of her name told me all I needed to know about Betty Norris's lifestyle. 'And Ruth Yates? Your sister?'

'Your sister was an artist, wasn't she?' asked Alf. 'A bit of a bohemian, I think they call them.'

'When they weren't calling her a slut,' said Mrs Higgins. 'The way the newspapers covered the case, well, they were not kind to Ruth and Betty. Made it seem like they deserved what happened to them. But I know you won't think like that, Bobbie. Will you look at the case for me? Please.'

I had no choice but to agree. I must admit my interest was piqued by what I had heard so far.

Mrs Higgins left and I had to get on with my work on the desk whilst Alf went back on the beat. Perhaps a look at the Ladykiller files would take my mind off Leo and my impending weekend away.

That was easier said than done, especially as he was waiting outside the station when I had finished my shift. His lovely eyes had dark circles underneath, and he looked more unkempt than usual. My Vespa was in the garage being mended, so Leo fell in behind me as I walked home.

'Bobbie, last night didn't quite go as I planned.'

'Have you changed your mind about going away?' I was surprised to find the thought of not going away with Leo hurt more than the thought of going.

'No, definitely not. I'm just sorry for you that it wasn't more romantic.'

'Well I didn't expect anything else in the Cunning Woman.'

'No, it's hardly the Ritz, is it? Let's go away together. It'll be great. We can see a show and take in the sights. And I promise that we'll have separate rooms and that nothing will happen unless you want it to.'

'Oh Leo . . . ' I swallowed back the lump in my throat.

He took my hand in his. 'I complained about you not showing your feelings last night, but I realise I'm not much better. I was clumsy and stupid in the way I asked you to come away. I didn't mean to make it sound so cheap, Bobbie, because that's not the way we are together. It's being here, I think, in Stony End, with everyone watching us. It's like living in a goldfish bowl. So let's go to London, and then we'll be away from here and the prying eyes. We can be ourselves then.'

'I'd really like that,' I said. Forgetting myself for a moment, I threw my arms around his neck in the middle of the street. 'I'd love it, in fact!' Things were going to be all right. We would have time alone to talk about our feelings and maybe, just maybe, he would ask

29

me to marry him. Perhaps the weekend away was a kind of audition.

'Doctor Stanhope! Bobbie!'

We turned to see Alf Norris tearing down the road on his bicycle, his face red and damp with perspiration. 'What is it?' I asked.

'They've found a body up at the castle.'

'Oh no,' I said, putting my hands to my mouth. 'Is it Dottie Riley?'

3

Stony End Castle overlooked the town from its vantage point high on a hill. The hamlet of Little Stony was just behind it. My last big case had taken me to Little Stony and the murder of an old man.

The victim, who was in the grounds of Stony End castle, was a woman of about thirty years of age. It was hard to tell from her bloated face, but I got the impression she had been quite attractive. Her hair was coiffured and she had a good figure, with long legs. Her clothes — a grey skirt suit and crisp white blouse — were well-cut. But the suit was generic, and I had one just like it. We found a label for a department store inside. Around her neck was a Paisley scarf.

'There's no identification,' said Alf as we waited for Detective Marshall to arrive. That would often take a while, as Marshall was prone to hangovers. 'I've already checked.'

'It looks as if she's been strangled,' said Leo, who had been examining the body. 'With her own scarf too. There doesn't seem to be any sign of sexual assault, but the autopsy will tell us more. I've never seen her before, and I know nearly everyone around here through my practice. Bobbie? Alf?'

We took a look at the woman's bloated face, but neither of us could see anything familiar about her. 'She's not a local,' Alf said.

I shook my head. 'I've never seen her in all the time I've lived in Stony End.' True I had only moved there the year before, but Stony End was a small town and everyone knew everyone else, if not by name then at least by sight. 'I could get in touch with the dress shop and find out who they sold the suit to.'

Alf nodded. 'Good idea. I should think the curator saw her too. Visitors have to pay to get in. Not that they always do. If they say they're using it as a cut through to the bowling green, they don't have to pay anything.'

The entry fee was nominal — about sixpence, which seems ridiculously cheap in retrospect, but at the time the castle was not cared for by any trust. As far as anyone knew, no kings had slept there and no battles had been fought from its walls, so it was of little historical interest. Yet the locals adored the place, and did all they could to maintain it. A group of local people, including builders, carpenters and other artisans, kept it upright in their spare time.

The castle had been built on the hillside, overlooking the valley. I looked out over the wall nearby, where there was a sheer twenty- to thirty-foot drop to the fields below. Certainly no one had carried her up that way, even using the trees that grew out of the lower wall.

'Old Mr Barker on the gate isn't always as sharp as he should be,' Leo said, as if reading my mind. 'When we were kids, we used to get in easily enough when he went off for his tea break. And let's just say that his tea was so potent he didn't always remember if we'd paid or not.'

'You were such a naughty boy,' I teased. Odd that I could joke about it now. Leo had been a real wild child, and completely different from the dedicated local doctor he had become.

'Then there are the tunnels leading to the catacombs,' he said, winking. 'They're on the east side of the castle, next to the river. A child under five feet tall can stand up in them and an adult could manage easily enough.'

'I'll go and talk to Mr Barker,' said Alf. 'You stay here and keep people away, Bobbie.'

'Okay, Alf.' I watched him walk away. 'I wonder where Dottie is,' I said to Leo. 'I was so afraid this would be her. Is it awful to feel relieved that it isn't?'

'No, of course not. Dottie is a local legend. Did you know that during the war she used to give out free fish and chips to those in need?'

'She was also a friend of Mum's,' I explained, 'so I didn't know how I was going to break it to Mum. And then there's poor Elvis . . . It is so odd that she took off and left him, Leo. She adores that dog. Something must have really rattled her.' I looked at the dead woman on the floor. 'She must be all right. She must be.'

Leo walked over and put his arm around my shoulder, kissing me on the forehead. 'She'll turn up. It's just a sad coincidence that we've found this woman when Dottie is missing. She's probably run off with Rock Hudson.'

I smiled. 'I think she likes James Garner more.'

'There you are then. Let's just hope that Doris Day doesn't scratch her eyes out.'

I laughed and put my head on his shoulder. It felt good to be back to normal with him again, after the awkwardness of the night before.

'When you two have finished smooching . . . ' said a tired-sounding voice from a few feet away.

'DS Marshall.' I almost stood to attention, and then remembered that Marshall did not much care for formality. It was a miracle the man was standing up straight. 'Alf has gone to speak to Mr Barker, the custodian.'

'What have we got then?'

Leo and I explained all that we had discovered.

'Good,' he said when we had finished. 'Blandford, you get back to the station and chase up that department store. Doctor, thank you for your time. The forensic team will be along soon.'

'Don't you want me to wait whilst you investigate?' I asked. 'To make sure no one disturbs the evidence.'

'No, it's fine. Alf will be back in a minute.'

I sighed. Marshall was not as hostile to me as some of the men at the station had been, but he still kept me out of the loop on murder cases, and always chose a male officer over me when it came to seeking help. No doubt he thought telephoning a dress shop was just within the limits of my capability.

With no choice but to obey my superiors, I started to leave the castle. Leo followed me with his hands in his pockets, whistling softly. He knew better than to speak to me when I was feeling downtrodden.

Alf Norris was still waiting at the curator's office, which was in a small lodge next to the castle gates. One of the windows doubled as a serving hatch through which people paid their money. Through the window one could see a small sitting room, with a fire with dying embers.

'Mr Barker has nipped into town for something,' he explained, pointing to a sign on the window which said 'Back in 5 minutes.'

'So the gate is open but no one is here to see who gets in or out,' I said. 'And everyone knows that five minutes is never just five minutes. Mr Barker only has to get caught in a queue at the post office or the fishmonger's. Or both.'

Alf nodded. 'Exactly, lass. I've been here ten minutes.'

'Perhaps it was Mr Barker,' said Leo. 'And he's done a runner.'

'Who murdered the woman?' I asked, aghast. I couldn't imagine old Mr Barker running anywhere. He had a gammy leg, as he was keen to remind everyone if he was asked to help out with local activities.

'An assignation that went wrong,' Alf suggested.

'But he's got to be eighty years old. I can't see him assignating with anyone.'

'Is assignating even a word?' asked Leo, mildly.

'It is now,' I said emphatically.

'Just because there's snow on the roof doesn't mean there isn't a fire in the grate.' Alf grinned, patting down his own greying locks.

'You old dog, Alf,' Leo laughed.

'Will you two show some decorum? A woman is dead.'

'Yes, of course. Sorry, darling.' Leo looked suitably abashed. 'It's just the thought of Mr Barker as a lothario . . . '

I suppressed a grin, not wanting to admit it was very unlikely. Also, the man himself was walking up the rise to the castle. Weighing at least eighteen stone and with a pronounced limp, carrying two string bags full of vegetables and other groceries, he was certainly no Gregory Peck. But stranger things had happened. The victim in the last murder I had investigated had been no oil painting, yet his lover had committed murder for him.

'I'd best be off,' said Leo. 'I still have my rounds to do.'

'Of course,' I said. 'Sorry to have kept you.'

'You can keep me anytime.' He kissed me on the cheek, and I could tell by the pressure of his lips that if Alf had not been there, the kiss would have been more passionate.

'What do you lot want?' asked Mr Barker, when he drew nearer, passing

Leo as he left the castle grounds and went back to his car. 'You needn't think you're getting free entry because you're in the police.'

'We've already been in, Mr Barker,' said Alf. 'So has half the town in the time you've been gone, I reckon. Are you aware there's a dead body on the grounds? Some kids phoned it in.'

'A dead what?'

'A body. A woman,' I said.

'Well don't look at me.'

'We need to know if you've seen anything,' Alf told him.

'When? When did she come in?'

'If we knew that, we wouldn't have to ask you,' said Leo.

'I thought you doctor types could tell how long someone has been dead.'

'Only in Agatha Christie novels. I'm afraid I have to work in the real world.'

We were getting nowhere, so I interrupted. 'She's in her forties, we think; a red-haired woman, wearing a grey suit. Like the one Kim Novak wore in Vertigo.'

'In what?'

'*Vertigo*? James Stewart? Alfred Hitchcock? Do you not go to the pictures, Mr Barker?'

'How can I when I'm stuck here all day?'

I bit my tongue so that I did not contradict him. 'Who has come in within the last couple of days? Do they have to sign in? Is there a book?'

'Have you got a warrant? I've seen Dixon of Dock Green. I know you've got to have one.'

'And you've got to stay on your post but you don't,' said Alf sternly. 'Now stop messing us around, Mr Barker, or we might have to take you down to the station for questioning. It's starting to look like you're stalling us.'

'All right, all right. Keep your hair on. There's no book. People don't have to sign in. They just give me their sixpence.'

'Don't they get a ticket?' I asked.

Mr Barker looked furtive. 'Most of the time.'

'Most of the time?'

'Well it depends how busy I am, doesn't it?'

Alf and I exchanged glances, both of us wondering if Mr Barker was creaming some off the top of the entry fees. He got free housing in the lodge and a small salary, but otherwise he was as poor as a church mouse. I could not say I blamed him and it was not why we were there. That was a problem for the castle committee.

'Have you been busy?' asked Alf.

'Not lately. That's why I was able to go out and do my shopping today. The weather's too cold so hardly anyone comes. Not that we're ever packed out here. Honestly, even in August I can sit here all day and not see a soul.'

'Can you remember who has been here?' I asked. I had my notebook out, poised and ready.

'Just some kids this morning, before school.'

'They'd be the ones who telephoned,' Alf said.

'They said they had homework to do on the history of the castle.'

'Probably came in to have a crafty fag, more like,' Alf suggested.

'Did you see a woman come in at all?' I asked. 'It might have been last night or yesterday afternoon. She might have had a man with her, or he came along afterwards.'

'The gates close at five o'clock, so no one would have come in after that,' Mr Barker said. He had put his shopping bags down and was rubbing his chin. The faint smell of whisky emanated from him.

'There are other ways into the castle, aren't there?'

'Yes, and I keep telling the committee, but they do nowt about it.'

'So kids get in?'

'They can get in for free anyway,' said Mr Barker. 'So they've no reason to break in, unless they want to mess around at night. I've sometimes had to chase them off. But I didn't see anyone last night. Kids are easy though, because even when they're trying to be quiet, they make a lot of noise.'

'So you didn't hear arguing or screaming?' I asked.

'No, nothing. I heard a car back-firing, but that was outside the gates, around nine o'clock last night.'

There did not seem to be much more that Mr Barker could tell us. It seemed to me that his little lodge was more of a cell, and that apart from the tiny window through which he took entry fees, he did not have much of a view of anything. It must have been a lonely hand-to-mouth life, for all that he lived in the pretty lodge of an ancient monument. I wondered how often he actually looked in the castle grounds. It was like owning a precious jewel. At first all you could do was admire it, but after a while it lost its lustre and was thrown into a box with all the other trinkets. The castle was pretty big as trinkets go, but even I forgot it was there sometimes.

'If you think of anything, give us a

ring at the station,' said Alf.

'Alf, I've got to go and see Elsie Atkins at the nursing home in Little Stony. I'll phone the department store headquarters when I get back to the station.'

'Is she still going on about that bike?'

'She is. It's my fault. I shouldn't have brought it up with her. It's just that it was one of Dad's cases before he died, so I wanted to try and solve it for him.'

'Go on then, lass.'

I kissed Leo goodbye and went to see Elsie Atkins.

The nursing home in Little Stony was a new addition to the hamlet. Up until a few months previously there had been no more than half a dozen houses and a derelict village hall. The village hall had been knocked down and a nursing home put in its place. Elsie Atkins was one of its first residents.

The home was a rather bland brick built building, with none of the character of the rest of the cottages in Little Stony. Elderly patients sat in the

45

grounds, despite the early spring chill in the air, whilst nurses wearing caps that looked like ships' sails bustled around them. Some of the elderly were quite sharp and aware, whilst others sat holding cups of tea as if they had no idea what to do with them. A sign on the wall next to the gate said that a garden fête would be held there at Whitsun to raise funds for the home. The gardens themselves were rather beautiful and well-kept.

I found Elsie Atkins sitting under the veranda. She was in a rocking chair and had a duck-egg-blue shawl around her shoulders, whilst her grey locks were piled on top of her hair, giving her the look of an aging goddess. She had clearly been a very good-looking woman in her youth.

'Oh you're not going to start us off about that bike again, are you?' asked one of the nurses. She was a stout middle-aged woman with a permanently harassed air about her. 'We've never shut up about it since the last time you came. Have we, Mrs Atkins?'

'Good morning, Mrs Atkins. I just thought I'd bring you up to date with my investigation.'

'You're Robert Blandford's girl,' said Mrs Atkins. Her eyes sparkled as if new life had come into them.

'That's right. I explained last time.'

'I'd know that red hair anywhere.'

'It came from my mother.'

'Of course, but you're still Robert's girl. Such a good man.'

I felt the same bittersweet pain that I always experienced when people talked about my father. He had been murdered when I was three years old, so I had not known him. Yet the people of Stony End who were old enough always spoke of him with reverence, and I only hoped I could be as good a police officer as he had been.

I took the empty seat next to Mrs Atkins, ignoring the 'tsk' of the nurse. 'We really ought to be getting our rest,' she said.

'Don't let me stop you,' said Mrs

Atkins. 'But perhaps you could bring us a cup of tea before you go.' Her eyes twinkled and I wondered just how vague she really was.

The nurse bustled away, muttering to herself.

'Now, about my bicycle,' she said.

'I have to be honest and say that I don't think we'll ever find it,' I explained. 'It's such a long time ago, and the trail really has run cold. In his notes my father put it down to children messing around.'

'Yes, I suppose so.'

'Mrs Atkins, do you mind if I ask you something?'

'Of course not, dear.'

'You seem like a very intelligent lady. Why are you worrying about your bicycle after all these years?'

'Oh, I don't know. Unfinished business, I suppose. Something about it bothered me, but I can't quite remember what it was or why I suddenly started worrying again. It's kind of you to say I'm intelligent, WPC Blandford, but the truth is it's all going away. Every morning when I wake up I've forgotten something important about my life. Yesterday it was my grandchildren's names. Today it was where I had put the gas bill.'

I frowned and looked over my shoulder at the building behind us. 'Do you have to pay the gas bill?'

'No, and that's the point. But for an hour this morning I was convinced that I had to and that if I did not, then we would all go cold and without food. The odd thing is that I never really knew what it was to go hungry. But I saw it, with the people I visited. I vowed that I would never get like that, and neither would my children.'

'On the night your bicycle was missing, where were you?'

'I was attending a birth. It was . . . ' The old lady sighed. 'See, there it goes again. I can't even remember who it was. And when I came out, my bicycle was gone. There was something else too about that night, but . . . oh I can't remember. But I can't help thinking that if we can find out what happened to my bicycle, it would bring it all back. My mind becomes darker with each passing day. I should like to know the truth before the light goes out completely.' She smiled sadly. 'Even if I do forget what that truth was.'

'I cannot promise anything.'

'I know, dear.'

'But I will keep asking. I'll go over Dad's notes again and see if I can find any clues. Is there anyone else I could talk to about that night?'

'I wish I could remember.'

'Of course.'

Without waiting for the nurse to bring a cup of tea, I said my goodbyes.

Being with Mrs Atkins and in that environment made me feel melancholy. Education had not come easy to me. I had struggled all the way through school, and whilst my grades had been good, I always believed it was some sort of fluke. Few girls were encouraged academically in those days so it was not surprising we fell into self-deprecation when we did do well. The idea of one day being an old lady and losing everything I had learned terrified me. Perhaps that is why I feel the need to write all this down now, before I lose it forever.

Mrs Atkins had been a pillar of her community and a woman whom everyone trusted with their very lives. Soon all her wisdom would be gone, leaving no more than an empty shell, like the others sitting in the care home. I shuddered and forced myself to think more positively. It did not have to be that way and if I could do anything to help her to remember, then I would.

It might only be a bicycle to some people, but to Elsie Atkins it was a key to opening up past memories. And who knew? It might even stave off the darkness.

Seeing her made me want to chat to my mum, so before I went back to the station, and because it was my lunch break anyway, I popped back to the cottage and gave her a call. She was nowhere near to Mrs Atkins's age, but at that time, God forgive me, fifty-two seemed ancient to me.

'Hello, Mum.'

'Oh, hello, Bobbie darling. Why aren't you at work?' Her voice had a strange, distant tone to it.

'It's nice to hear from you too, Mum!'

'Of course it's nice to hear from you, love. I'm just about to sit down to lunch though.'

'I'm on my lunch break. I just wanted to hear your voice, that's all.'

'Why? What's happened?'

It would be hard to explain about the dead woman in the castle and Mrs Atkins's bike. My mother had not approved of my career. It was even harder to discuss my troubles with Leo. I did not think she would understand, because I could not conceive of her being young and having romantic troubles.

'Oh nothing. Just one of those days. We've got a dog.'

'Oh.'

'Yes, it's Dottie Riley's. She's gone missing and left her dog, Elvis, behind.'

'That's very strange.' I heard someone talking in the background. 'I'm sorry, Bobbie, but lunch is getting cold.'

'Are you with someone, Mum?'

'I do have a guest, yes.'

'A boyfriend?' My incredulity must have been obvious.

'Why shouldn't I have a boyfriend, Bobbie? Your father has been gone a long time now.'

'I know, Mum. It's just that you hadn't said anything.'

'And how long was it before you told me about that young doctor?'

'I wanted to be sure.'

'Then you'll perhaps understand that I might want to be sure as well.'

'Okay, Mum.' Not for the first time, I marvelled at my mother's ability to reduce me to a five-year-old. The telephone table seemed to grow to twice the size, and the handset felt huge in my hands. 'I hope you have a nice lunch and that I get to meet him one day.'

I put the phone down and sat on the bottom step of the staircase. My first thought was: Mum with a boyfriend. That's a new thing. My second thought was: How could she? Did my father mean so little to her?

You do not have to tell me I was being irrational and unfair on my mother. I already knew that. But for so long there had been no one in Mum's life except me and my brother, Tom. Indignation and perhaps a little bit of jealousy washed over me. Not least because my mother was not available to talk to me as I always expected her to be. A man had taken my place at her table and perhaps even in her heart.

Why now, after all this time? And why had she not told me about him?

* * *

A telephone call to the headquarters of the department store, when I returned to the station, yielded the information that hundreds of the grey skirt-suits had been sold in its department stores, but that it would be impossible to say which without a receipt or the original packaging.

'The receipt would state which store and the original packaging would have a factory number on it,' explained the woman on the other end of the telephone.

'There would be nothing on the clothing itself?' I asked.

'I'm afraid not. Our labels are very discreet.' This was in the days when people would not dream of wearing the labels on the outside. Discretion was the order of the day.

'Is there any way of narrowing it down?'

'I can tell you that all our department stores are in the north. We have more than twenty stores in County Durham, Teesside, Cumbria, Yorkshire — East and West Riding, Lincolnshire, Nottinghamshire and Derbyshire. Our flagship store is in Scarborough.'

'Derbyshire,' I said. 'So she could be

local after all,' I mused, more to myself than to anyone. 'Well thank you very much for your help.'

'There is one other thing that may help,' the woman said before I could hang up the telephone.

'What is that?'

'The suit of which you speak was part of a promotion late last year involving trading stamps. Customers who saved up enough stamps could buy the suit for half price. I'm not sure if your victim would have done that, but it might narrow things down as the offer was only on at our Scarborough store to celebrate our opening in eighteen eighty-one.'

'Thank you, you've been most helpful.'

'Basically,' I told Alf Norris and the sarge over a cup of tea later, 'if we find Green Shield Stamps in her pockets, we've cracked it. But it might explain why she was dressed so well. We could send her picture up to the store in Scarborough and see if anyone recognises her.'

'It's a bit of a long shot,' said the sarge. 'She could have bought the suit at any one of those twenty-odd stores, and she could have bought it last week for all we know. We can't go off on some wild goose chase because a suit that was bought by thousands of women might have been on sale in Scarborough last year. Let's see what her autopsy brings up, and have a look into missing persons. Someone will be wondering where she is.'

4

As the weeks passed by, and spring turned to summer, it seemed that no one wondered where our victim was. She did not turn up on any missing person's lists, and we could find no dental or medical records with her name on them. That was not unusual. Some people never visited the dentist, and as the autopsy showed that the woman had not had any major surgeries, there was nothing to search for in medical records. It was proved that she had been strangled with her own scarf, as Leo had already ascertained, but there were no other marks on her body.

'It's almost as if she stood there and let him do it,' I said to the sarge when the team met to discuss unsolved cases. 'You'd think if someone got hold of your scarf and started to tighten it, you'd push them away.'

'Unless he took her by surprise,' said the sarge. 'What else have we got?'

'I still haven't found out anything about Mrs Atkins's bicycle.'

The sarge sighed. 'That's hardly a priority, Blandford.'

'It is for her,' I replied. 'She's not getting any younger and her memory is getting worse. I just want to do this one thing for her.'

'We'll just call you Donna Quixote, shall we? Tilting at windmills . . . '

The sarge surprised me sometimes. Mostly he was just a normal bloke in his early fifties who liked a bourbon biscuit with his tea and a pint at the end of the day. He was not bad-looking for his age, and I knew a few of the women in Stony End would have liked to set their cap at him. He lived alone in a cottage attached to the station and showed every signs of becoming a grumpy old man. But every so often he would prove himself to be very well-read and display a wit that caught everyone off guard.

He had been one of my dad's best friends, but whilst dad had stayed in Stony End during the war due to medical reasons, the sarge had gone off to join the fighting. He never talked about the war and his place in it, but it was well known that his wife, whom he had expected to wait for him, had gone off to America with an airman.

'Somebody has to bring those windmills under control, Sarge,' I said, ignoring the chuckles of the rest of my colleagues.

'And it'd take a Blandford to do it,' said the sarge. 'Your dad had a touch of the Don Quixote about him, but he was better at picking his campaigns. Now, what have we next? And if anyone tells me that Mrs Higgins's cabbages have gone missing again, I may throw you all out.'

I blushed scarlet. In my first year as a probationer, I had made much of Mrs Higgins's missing cabbages. No one had taken much notice of me, even though I had been right to investigate. I imagined that Mrs Atkins's missing bicycle would join the list of 'Daft things WPC Blandford got herself into'. I almost reminded the sarge that the missing bike had been one of my dad's campaigns, but I did not want to encourage any more derision on the part of my workmates. It was hard enough being the only woman in the police station.

There was more talk about other cases, and the missing Dottie Riley. 'It's all been sorted,' said Detective Sergeant Marshall, drinking from his teacup as if his life depended on it. His hands shook, and we all knew they would not stop shaking until he had managed to get his first drink of the day. 'She's phoned her sister and said she's taking a bit of a break. Her sister has taken over the running of the chip shop for now, which suggests that she knows something she's not telling us. But the sister is not creaming off the books or trying to claim the rest of Mrs Riley's money. I've asked Dottie's sister to tell her to get in touch with us so we can stop wasting time worrying about her.'

'I reckon Dottie has gone off with some man,' said Alf.

There were nods of agreement all around. Only I felt uneasy about it, as it seemed so out of character. Leaving Elvis behind made it seem very unlikely. He was still living with me and Annabel, and had become a part of the family. We had offered him to Dottie's sister, but she had taken one look at him and said with a shudder, 'No thank you.'

The talk turned to the weekend roster. 'Who is on duty?' asked the sarge. 'Remember that Alf here has to go and have his ingrown toenail sorted on Friday, so I need volunteers. Blandford?'

'Oh . . . sorry, Sarge. I can't. I'm going away for the weekend.' This was another cue for me to turn a shade of scarlet.

'Just what the doctor ordered,' said one of the men to raucous laughter.

'Enough!' said the sarge. 'What WPC

Blandford does with her weekends is her own business. No doubt the rest of you will just be getting hammered in the pub.' He pointed to two of the men and ordered them to take it in turns to cover Alf's shift.

When the meeting was over, we all started to pile out. 'Blandford,' said the sarge as I moved towards the door, 'come back in and shut the door.'

I feared a dressing-down for something I had done. Or not done.

'So you're definitely going away this weekend?'

'Yes, Sarge. It's all arranged. We're going to see Anthony Newley in *Stop the World I Want to Get Off*.'

'Blandford, the days when sergeants interfered in the private lives of police officers, telling them who they could marry and all that, have long gone. But I'd be failing in my duty if I didn't warn you about the way people are talking. You and Doctor Stanhope are both over twenty-one, but you're also considered pillars of this community. Any scandal could ruin that, and take away any sense of authority you might have.'

'Are you saying I shouldn't go this weekend, Sarge?'

'It's not my place to say so. You've already heard the way the men are snickering. Are you sure you can cope with what comes afterwards? They might think that you're a . . . a sure thing . . . lass.'

'But I'm not. I love Leo and he . . . ' I floundered there. I could not say that Leo loved me, because he had not said it.

'You'll do what you want, no matter what I say. I'm just warning you of the consequences.'

'Will I lose my job?' I asked, starting to worry.

'No. But . . . ' It was the sarge's turn to look awkward. 'If your father was here, or your mother, they could warn you about these things, but there are consequences when two people . . . get together. You may have no choice but to give up your job. If you . . . you know.'

'Become pregnant?'

'Yes.'

'I've no intentions of doing that, Sarge. I've not even decided if . . . if we . . . ' The conversation was getting more and more awkward. 'I mean, I don't have to do anything.'

'Whether you do or not, people will think that you have.'

'That's their business, Sarge. I'm not responsible for what people think.'

'Actually I think you are, Blandford. If you go away this weekend, then it will be talked about. People are talking about it now, but it's all to play for, as they say.'

'Has Mum been talking to you?' I asked.

'Dina might have said something.'

'Well, Mum is in no position to judge. Every time I telephone, she's with that man. I phoned the other night at midnight and he was obviously still there.'

'I see.' For some reason the sarge looked unhappy. 'I see. Well, you know best.'

I was of the mind that people should grow up, but the sixties had not yet begun to swing — they hardly reached that status at all in a town like Stony End. I pushed aside any doubts that I had. Things would turn spectacularly bad, but not in any of the ways I had expected.

When I left the sarge's office, Mrs Higgins was waiting for me in reception. 'I wondered if you'd had a look at my sister's murder yet, WPC Blandford.' I thought I had stopped being surprised by Mrs Higgins's attire, but that day she wore a yellow sou'wester, a thick Arran sweater and wellington boots, as if she expected to be sent to sea at the earliest opportunity. Outside the weather was seventy degrees, so goodness knew how hot she was. It made me perspire just to look at her.

Shame overwhelmed me. I had completely forgotten. The truth was that a recent murder always took precedence over unsolved cases. A current murder meant that the murderer could strike again. Cold cases tended to suggest that the murderer had either given up or died. But I had also spent a lot of time on Mrs Atkins's bicycle, due to the urgency of helping that lady. I did not think Mrs Higgins was going to die. She was quite a bit younger than Mrs Atkins. But she was considered a bit unstable. This was the result of her husband having had her sectioned, just so he could take her money and run off with his lover. She had been what one might call 'normal' before entering the sanatorium, but whatever had happened to her in there had left her slightly unhinged.

'Not yet, Mrs Higgins. We've been rather busy.'

'I know. Another dead woman. But that was months ago. It was probably those commies I told you about.'

'Sorry, that also slipped my mind.' In truth I had ignored the bit about the commies, putting it down to Mrs Higgins watching too many spy dramas on television. *Danger Man* was a favourite and the recent Bay of Pigs incident had everyone worried about communists, believing that they were about to have their liberty taken away by Marxists who, for some reason, always chose to live in free countries and not those places that had already converted to communism. 'I'll go take a look at the files now, and come and see you after work. Is that all right?'

She nodded curtly and left the station. I was not worried that she had fallen out with me. Mrs Higgins was not that sort of woman. She just said what she thought, and then moved on.

I made my way down to the cellar, which I had turned into an office for myself. I did not get much time to use it, due to my other duties, but when things were quiet I liked to go down there and look through the cases. I had been doing it for over a year, yet had barely touched the surface. There were cases going back to the late nineteen-hundreds but not all of them were in alphabetical or file number order.

I had not even begun to search for

the files related to Ruth Yates and Betty Norris. It took me a while, but I finally tracked them down. They had been kept in different file boxes, which seemed odd if the murders were thought to be connected. Brushing the dust from my hands, I sat down and began to read.

Ruth Yates, Mrs Higgins's sister, had been a Bohemian type, according to reports. She painted and sculpted, but not very successfully by all accounts. She had been found dead in the local hotel, which was now a hostel. The cause of death was strangulation. I stopped there. Had I known that? I flicked through the notes quickly and found out that not only had Ruth Yates been strangled, but she had been strangled with her own scarf. Just like our anonymous victim. She had been thirty-two years old when she died.

I quickly read the files relating to Betty Norris. Betty, according to the notes, had a difficult life. I remember Alf telling me that he had struggled as a child and the police force had saved him. It seems that he and his cousin came from a family of ne'er-do-wells. Alf had escaped that life, but Betty had a record a mile long for prostitution, shoplifting and other petty offences. She had been thirty-three when she died. She too had been strangled with her own scarf.

I looked through the list of belongings for the two women. Both had owned a Paisley scarf. It was too much of a coincidence to ignore.

'Sarge!' I called, running up the stairs with the files in my hands. 'Sarge! You need to see this!'

5

'Can you tell me more about Ruth, Mrs Higgins?' I asked. I sat on one side of the dinette in her caravan. She had made a date and walnut cake and had put a cup of hot tea next to it. I had a feeling she had been expecting me to call. 'I've read the notes, but it isn't the same. You said that the papers suggested she was a . . . '

'A slut. That's what they all said.'

'They?'

'The police, the newspapers. They all made that assumption. Ruth was always a bit flighty, but not in the sense they believed. She was artistic, and it made her a bit dreamy. Imagination was frowned upon in our family.'

I wanted to suggest how hard that must have been for Mrs Higgins too, but I needed to keep her on target or I would be there all night.

'It also made her a bit gullible,' Mrs Higgins continued. 'A man need only cite a bit of poetry to her and she fell for him in a big way. All her romances were true romances. At least in her head.'

'She never married?'

'No. The men always left her.'

'Was there a man in her life at the time of her death?'

'I suppose there might have been. There usually was. She had a thing about a man in uniform and with a posh accent.'

'But you don't have a name?'

Mrs Higgins thought about it for a while. 'Oh, I don't know. I was incarcerated at the time so I don't really remember. The police came to speak to me then but I could not tell them much. She wrote to me, and I think she mentioned a name like Harold or Arthur York, but I had ripped all my letters in a fit of pique. Angry, I suppose, at being there whilst she was out having a life.'

Knowing the pain of Mrs Higgins's past in the sanatorium, I thought it better to move on. 'It says she was an artist and sculptor.'

Mrs Higgins scoffed. 'She wanted to be, and her drawings weren't bad, but she had ideas beyond her talents. Let me show you. You'll have to get up.'

The next few minutes were spent rearranging the caravan so that Mrs Higgins could get into the storage space under the seating. All the cups and saucers had to go on the miniscule worktop. The cake was put in the sink, which was thankfully empty of dishes and water, and other odds and ends were spread across the floor. Finally, after much rummaging — I wondered how she managed to fit so much in such a confined space — Mrs Higgins pulled out a black portfolio.

'This isn't everything. The rest is in storage. And some were sold to pay for the family lawyer who had to speak for us during the investigation. Her paintings brought quite good sums for a while after her murder. Everyone wanted a piece of the macabre. But I kept these, and I wouldn't let my mother sell them.'

The paintings were not bad at all, though I was not an expert. One was of a kingfisher wading in a pool. Others were more sketches than finished paintings of flora and fauna, like you see in encyclopaedias and nature books. One particularly striking sketch was of a young woman in Edwardian dress stretched out on a chaise longue.

'She wanted to work in illustrating,' said Mrs Higgins. 'Instead she got a job at Pearson's Pottery in Chesterfield, decorating the cups. She didn't stick that for long. She moved to London, thinking to find her fortune there, but she only got a similar job there, working on tourist tat. Half the time she had to write to Mother or myself for money for food and lodgings. We'd both send her something and that would keep her going for a while. Well, you look after family, don't you? Occasionally she would find a man who would pay these things for her, but as I said, it never lasted. But she was not a prostitute or a slut. Not like they said in the press. If a man had been murdered and it was found he had been with several women, no one would judge him.'

'What was she doing in Stony End?' I asked.

'She had come up to visit me. It was when my husband put me in the sanatorium and she was going to come and speak up for me, to tell them that I was not mad. I didn't even see her. On the day she was supposed to come, I had done some silly thing that ended with them giving me knock-out drops. It sometimes makes you act mad, when you're trying to prove you're not.' Mrs Higgins's eyes darkened. My heart ached for the pain she must have endured. 'Before she could try another visit, she was dead.'

'I'm so sorry.'

'No use being sorry now. It was a long time ago.'

'Yet you want to reopen the case, Mrs Higgins.'

'I do. I'm not getting any younger and I'd like to think her killer was behind bars.'

'Do you know anything about whom she might have seen whilst she was visiting?'

'No. My mother might have, but she's long dead. I wasn't a resident then — except up at the sanatorium, so I don't know who my sister knocked around with.'

'I'll ask around,' I promised.

'So why are you interested now,' she asked me, 'when you haven't bothered for months?'

'I'm not supposed to say until we know for definite.'

'It's the woman who was killed up at the castle, isn't it?'

'She was strangled with her Paisley scarf, like your sister and Betty Norris.'

'I see,' said Mrs Higgins, pursing her lips.

'I know you'll think it's unfair that we haven't paid more attention to your sister's death, but we will now we've found a connection, I promise.'

'That's not what I'm getting at. They said that Ruth had on a Paisley scarf.

She would never have worn Paisley. She hated it.'

When I left Mrs Higgins, I rode my Vespa to the Springfield Estate on the outskirts of town. It was a warm summer evening, and I wished the ride could go on forever.

Greta and Alf Norris lived in a prefab on the estate. Greta was Austrian, and Alf had met her during the war when it had been his job to keep an eye on foreign nationals. It had almost ruined his career when he married her, but he had stood his ground and Greta herself had proved to be the perfect policeman's wife.

'Bobbie,' said Greta, when she opened the door. 'You should have said you were coming. Baking day is not until tomorrow and I have nothing to offer you.' Her accent was so slight that unless told she was Austrian, few people guessed it.

I assured her that Mrs Higgins had already taken care of my sweet tooth. 'I'm actually here to see Alf on official business.' Alf had been on his beat when I had made the connection between the murders, and the sarge had asked me to speak to him.

'Come in, come in. I'm sure I can find you a bit of cake somewhere. Let it not be said that Martha Higgins is a better hostess than me.' Ignoring my protests, she showed me into her neat little sitting room, telling me to sit down, and then bustled around in the kitchen. There was a serving hatch between the kitchen and living room. 'Alf is up at the cemetery,' she called through the hatch. 'It would have been his mother's birthday today.'

'I actually came to talk to him about Betty Norris,' I said.

'Oh, his fiancée. That was so tragic.'

'No, not his fiancée. His cousin. Was his fiancée murdered too? No one told me.'

I walked over to the hatch, but Greta was already on her way from the kitchen, and she pushed the sitting room door open whilst carrying a tea tray. 'I found some malt loaf,' she said with a smile.

'Not homemade of course, but we can't have you going hungry.' She put the tray down on the coffee table.

The possibility of me going hungry in Stony End was highly unlikely. Everyone I knew insisted on feeding me. It was lucky I did so much walking on the beat, or it would have been hard to stay fit and healthy. Plus I was young and the young burn calories so easily.

'We seem to be talking at cross purposes, Greta,' I said. 'I was talking about Alf's cousin, Betty. You mentioned his fiancée.'

'I know who Betty was,' said Greta with a smile. 'Alf and I have no secrets. He and Betty were engaged for a short time before the war.'

'But they were first cousins, weren't they?'

'Such a thing is not illegal or particularly rare, dear child. Most of the royal houses of Europe are the result of cousins marrying. I don't say there was any great passion between Alf and Betty. At least not the way he tells it. I think he cared about her and wanted to save her from the life she was leading.'

It changed things considerably. Alf had not told me he and Betty had been engaged on the day Mrs Higgins first brought up the subject. In fact he had made a point of saying that they were not close. An engagement suggested they had been very close indeed, even if Alf had only offered to marry his cousin out of chivalry.

As I tried to nibble at the buttered malt loaf that Greta pressed on me, my stomach began to churn. Alf was like a favourite uncle to me, and had been one of my first friends at the station. Why would he lie to me?

'Which cemetery has Alf gone to?' I asked when I had managed to swallow one slice. Normally I adored buttered malt loaf, but I was full from Mrs Higgins's cake and upset by what I had found out.

'The one behind St Jude's,' Greta said.

'I'll go and see if I can find him. Thank you for the malt loaf and tea, Greta.'

'You come again the day after tomorrow, and I will have the best cake ever waiting for you. I will need the company when Alf is in hospital, having his toenail treated.'

'I'm going to London on Friday evening,' I said, feeling the heat rise to my cheeks.

'Ah, yes, so I have heard.' Greta appeared about to say something, but clamped her lips shut.

I waited but she seemed determined not to pass judgement on my weekend. 'Thank you, Greta.' Impulsively I kissed her on the cheek. If Alf was my favourite uncle, Greta was my favourite aunt.

I found Alf sitting on a bench in the cemetery. I sat next to him and looked in the direction in which he did. It was not his mother's grave that he was visiting. The tombstone opposite said:

Elizabeth Norris
1909–1939
Into thy Father's Arms

'They didn't want to bury her in here,' Alf said before I could speak, 'because of what she had been and despite how she lost her life. The family had to remind them all of Mary Magdalene.'

'Why didn't you tell me you were engaged to her, Alf?' I asked. 'You said you weren't close, but you must have been.' I didn't tell him that Greta had told me. I didn't have to. He and Greta were so finely tuned to each other, he would have guessed it. Nor would he reproach her for telling me. I often dreamed that one day Leo and I would have the same type of love.

'Shame I suppose, lass. Because of what she'd made of her life. And because nowadays it's frowned upon for cousins to marry, even though it's not illegal. Our lives, as children, left a lot to be desired. Our fathers were brothers, and wrong 'uns both of them. They were involved in all sorts of scams and cons. But Betty's father was wrong in other ways. She didn't tell me everything, but enough for me to know that he had destroyed her long before she set upon her own path of self-destruction. So I thought I could save her, help her to be respectable, make her feel some pride in herself. I asked nothing of her. She went along with it for a while. But the pain in her was too deep, and she sought solace in the bottle and in other men who treated her just as badly as my uncle did. She ended the engagement and then took up her place on the town hall steps with Pearl and her girls.'

'I'm so sorry, Alf.' I put my hand in his.

'It's happening again, isn't it? I thought so when we found that woman in the castle grounds, but I didn't want to believe it.'

'The modus operandi seems to be the same,' I said, taking some solace in being able to speak professionally rather than personally. 'They were all strangled with a Paisley scarf. Mrs Higgins tells me that her sister would never have worn one. Do you remember if Betty owned one?'

'I'm sorry, lass, but I wouldn't know what she owned and what she didn't. It's the sort of thing other women notice, but not men. Greta says she could walk around in a sack and I'd never know. Mind you, she always just looks beautiful to me.'

I smiled and squeezed his hand. 'If you remember anything, Alf . . . '

'I know, lass. I'll tell you.'

'Do you know if there was a particular man that she saw often?'

Alf shrugged. 'As you know, we weren't from Stony End originally,' he said. 'We came from Tansley. I wasn't even at this station to begin with. Then I met Greta and that upset my sergeant, so I was sent here. It was a coincidence that I found myself here, where my cousin had been murdered. Pearl is the one you need to speak to.'

I agreed with that, but felt emotionally wrung out, so I decided to go home and leave Pearl for another day.

'It's so sad,' I told Annabel over a cup of Horlicks. We sat curled up in front of the hearth, even though it was too warm for a fire. 'Ruth Yates was a talented artist, but she just didn't have that spark to make the big time. People called her names because she had a few lovers, but if she'd been a man no one would have batted an eyelid. Betty Norris had been abused by men all her life, except for dear old Alf, and she couldn't even imagine herself being a respected policeman's wife. It makes me wonder . . . '

'Wonder what, sweetie?'

'Whether I should go away with Leo this weekend.'

'You don't think you're going to end up murdered just because of a dirty weekend in London, do you, darling?'

'No, but a woman's reputation matters, doesn't it? Much more so than a man's. I've already made one mistake with the Italian.' The Italian had been a man whom I had an affair with before moving to Stony End. I did not know till it was too late that he was already married. He was one of the reasons I had taken things so slowly with Leo. I did not want to be a slave to my passions. 'And you've just said it. A 'dirty weekend' in London. It all makes it sound so cheap, and yet for me it'll be a big step in my relationship with Leo.'

'So don't go.'

'But if I don't, we'll still be where we are now. I sometimes feel as if life has stopped still. I'm still on probation at the station, and sometimes I feel as if I'm still on probation with Leo.'

'You think sleeping with him will make you closer?'

'It might.'

'And it might just make you feel cheap.'

'Annabel! I didn't know you thought like that!'

'Oh I don't. It's up to you and I am

in no position to judge. I'm just basing it on personal experience. I did exactly the same thing. I let myself go with a man thinking it would take our relationship to the next level. Marriage, to be blunt. But it didn't. He'd just got what he wanted, and I was left feeling cheap and nasty. You may think I'm sophisticated where men are concerned, but I'm just as capable of getting it wrong, darling.'

'I had no idea.'

'I'm not saying you shouldn't go away with Leo. I'm just saying that you need to be sure it's for the right reasons. Go because you want to go to London and have some fun. Not because you think he will immediately propose to you.'

'I don't. I mean . . . ' But that was what I had been thinking; if Leo and I became intimate he would want to marry me. I took a sip of Horlicks, wishing it was something stronger. 'I really don't know what to do now.'

6

On Saturday evening, Leo and I walked hand in hand down Shaftesbury Avenue in London. I held my head high. I was a modern woman and completely sure that this was where I should be. If there were still some nagging doubts, Leo had kissed them away when he had picked me up from the cottage on the Friday afternoon.

I wanted him and he wanted me, and what others thought did not matter. I had to admit it was easier the further away we got from Stony End and those who might watch and judge us. In London nobody knew who we were. All they saw was a good-looking young couple enjoying each other's company.

'There it is,' he said, pointing. 'The Queen's Theatre.' The marquee displayed the title of the play, *Stop the World I Want to Get Off*, with the names of the stars, Anthony Newley and Anna Quayle. The theatre had been bombed during the war and had only recently been rebuilt and refurbished, so it had the effect of looking both historical and fresh at the same time. I tingled with excitement. I had only ever been to local amateur dramatics society plays. This was the first time I would see a play in the West End and with big-named stars.

'Shall we get dinner first, darling?'

'Yes, please.'

We found a steak house that catered for the theatre crowd, ensuring that all courses were served before the curtain rose. We both had prawn cocktail, steak and chips and black forest gateau, followed by Irish coffee.

'Leo,' I said as I sipped my coffee, relishing the creamy top layer as it caressed my tongue, 'I'm sorry. About last night.'

'I've already told you, it doesn't matter.'

'I just had an attack of nerves, that's all.'

He reached across and put his hand

over mine. 'If truth be known, I was a bit nervous myself. It was probably best that we both got a good night's sleep without feeling we have to . . . perform.'

I giggled. 'It's not as if I'm . . . well, you know. I mean, you do know, don't you? About the Italian?'

'Yes, I know some of it, which is why I understand you don't want to make a mistake again.'

'I wouldn't call you a mistake, Leo. Not ever. You're the best thing that's ever happened to me.'

He smiled, and it lit up his handsome face. 'The feeling is mutual. Tell me about the Italian. Maybe we can put some ghosts to rest.'

'He was not handsome. Not in the way you are,' I explained. 'But he had that foreign charm. You know the type. Very attentive and capable of making you feel as if you were the only person in the room. I was eighteen when we met and ready to believe anything he told me. He said that his family had left Italy before the war, on the run from

Mussolini. Or it might have been the mafia. Now I come to think of it, the story did change somewhat with each telling!' I laughed. 'I must have had 'gullible' stamped across my forehead. I used to have fantasies of being the one to save him from the mafia.'

'Or Mussolini.'

'Exactly! I'd be very brave and plucky and then he would be grateful and m-marry me . . . ' I faltered slightly, remembering my conversation with Annabel. I did not want to make it too obvious to Leo that I had marriage on my mind. 'His tales became taller, but I was stupid and believed everything he told me. Including that he loved me and did want to m-marry me. So I erm . . . gave in to him. I don't want to seem like the victim here, Leo. I knew what I was doing. He might have fooled me in lots of ways, but I was sure I wanted to . . . you know.'

'I know. And I don't want details. I'm not that masochistic. What happened then?'

'My boss — I was working in a hotel

at the time — called us in because there was a discrepancy in the accounts. That was when it all came out, because the Italian had been sending money to his wife, and the boss wanted to know how he could afford to. I instantly blew a fuse so blurted out about our relationship and I was fired on the spot. Oh the Italian got to keep his job — it turned out another member of staff was stealing — but I was considered damaged goods and not suitable for such a fine establishment. Then I joined the police force, and the rest, as they say, is history. Men always come out of these things better. It's like the case we're on at the moment. You know, with the woman found in the castle grounds?'

'Yes.'

'I've been talking to Mrs Higgins and Alf about her sister and his cousin, and both women were vilified and treated as if they were nothing. It might explain why no one really bothered with the case at the time. No one cared about what were seen as good-time girls. So it made me even more nervous about this weekend. So much is at stake, Leo. My reputation more than yours.'

'You know, I hope, that I will always protect you. I won't let anyone say anything about you, Bobbie.'

'Bless you for that. The thing is, now we've come away together, they'll believe we did anyway, won't they?'

'They might, but we're not responsible for what other people believe.'

'Oh, but we are, Leo. Just by spending the weekend away together. Tongues were wagging before we came. Who knows what will be said when we return? So it makes me think that at least if we don't . . . Well, at least we'll know we didn't. Does that make sense?'

'Not a bit of it, but if it makes you happy, then I'm on your side all the way.'

'Why do I think you're only saying the right things so that you can seduce me?'

Leo laughed. 'I just can't win, can I?'

I smiled back. 'You already have won,

in more ways than you know.'

We left the restaurant and went to the show. Anthony Newley played a lothario and told the tale of all the women he had known, including his wife. At crucial points in the play he would shout 'Stop the world, I want to get off' and tell the audience the story. I understood how he felt. Haven't we all wanted to stop the world for a few moments, either to get our breath back, or to savour the moment for a little bit longer? On that night, I definitely wanted to savour the moments with Leo. By the end, when Newley sang 'What Kind of Fool Am I?', I was in tears and came away humming the songs.

We walked along the embankment in the moonlight, chatting quietly about the show and life in general. Stony End, with its wagging tongues, seemed a million miles away. Other couples walked ahead or behind us, all lost in their own worlds.

'Do you know, this is the first time we've been able to spend time together without you being called off to deliver a baby or me being called to sort out a fight in the pub?' I said to Leo, putting my head on his shoulder.

'Yes, we give so much to that town,' he said, kissing me on the top of my head. 'It's nice to be just us, Leo and Bobbie.'

If truth be known, it actually felt a little bit unreal. I was not really Bobbie and he was not Leo. At least not as the people in Stony End knew us. We were just another anonymous couple walking in the moonlight, with no one to judge us. For all anyone knew, we were married. Unless they looked specifically at my ring finger. Talking about my fears to Leo had brought them into the open and helped me to push them aside. What had I to be afraid of?

I stopped and turned to him, putting my arms around his neck and pulling him closer. I could feel his warm breath on my cheek. My whole body began to tingle. 'Leo?'

'What, darling?'

'I don't feel nervous anymore.'

His lips found mine and we shared a long and luxurious kiss as the River Thames swept along behind us, leading out into the sea. I imagined all our hopes and dreams riding on it, taking them to a strange land where no one could judge.

We were quiet on the walk back to the hotel.

'Are you sure?' he asked when we reached the door to my room.

'Absolutely certain.' I took his hand and pulled him inside.

★ ★ ★

I felt a little shy on the train trip back to Stony End. Leo had behaved as a complete gentleman, taking special care of me after we had made love, and stemming my worries about him not respecting me. He left my room early so that the maid would not know he had been there, and at breakfast time he accompanied me downstairs.

If I was a little disappointed, it had

nothing to do with the love-making. That had been wonderful, and everything I had dreamed it would be. It was that Leo had not proposed to me, as I had hoped he would. I chided myself for behaving like a love-struck school-girl. This was not some romantic novel or film. This was real life, and in real life things did not happen exactly when and how you wanted them to.

'Are you all right?' Leo asked for about the tenth time that morning. He took my hand as I gazed out of the train window.

'Yes, I'm fine.'

'You've been very quiet all morning.'

'I've had a lot to think about,' I replied coquettishly, trying not to let my disappointment spoil the whole weekend.

'Bobbie . . . ' he said in a tentative tone.

'Yes, Leo?' Was this it? Was this the moment he would ask me to marry him?

'Perhaps we could make a regular

thing of it. Going down to London and getting away from the madding crowd. As they say.'

I sighed but managed to turn it into a happy sigh, followed by a smile, despite the heavy weight on my chest. 'Yes, yes, that would be nice.'

'Something is wrong,' he said. 'I can tell.'

'No, no, nothing is wrong. Honestly, what could be?' I lowered my voice. 'Was last night not good for you?'

'Last night was incredible,' he said, squeezing my hand. 'I just have a feeling you were expecting more. Bobbie, I really meant to say . . . '

'Tickets please!'

Almost as if we had been caught in a compromising situation on the train, we both sat up straight, letting go of each other's hands. 'Here you are,' said Leo, handing over both tickets.

Whatever Leo had been going to say was lost in the awkwardness of the moment and we did not speak again until we said goodbye at my front door.

'Well?' said Annabel, jumping up from the sofa. Elvis ran to greet me, plonking his wet nose on my hand. 'Tell me. Tell me!'

'It was lovely. We had a lovely time.'

'Lovely . . . ' said Annabel, frowning. 'I'm guessing there was no proposal.'

'No, but he didn't make me feel cheap either. Honestly, Annabel, he was . . . '

'Lovely?'

'Yes,' I said curtly, before running upstairs with my suitcase.

I will not cry, I told myself as I unpacked my clothes and sorted out what needed to go in the wash. *I will not spoil what has been a special weekend. I would behave like a mature, sophisticated woman. Leo must never know what I hoped.* Perhaps it was too soon anyway, I told myself. Although we had known each other for a year and a half, a lot of that time had been spent apart, both literally and figuratively. We had really only been in a steady relationship for a few months. But it was not just that he had not asked me to marry him. He had still not told me he loved me, not even when we were at our most intimate. What if he just saw me as someone to have a good time with? What if my experience with the Italian had given Leo that impression? He may not have made me feel cheap, but I feared that I had cheapened myself.

Such worries might seem ridiculous to twenty-first century women who are not judged on their love lives, but back then it mattered. As I had told Leo: a woman's reputation was sometimes all she had. A man might be an absolute rotter with women, but if he was successful in his career it did not matter. I could be the best police-woman in the world — though I was often far from it — but one mistake in my private life could ruin me. I had already survived one such mistake, with the Italian, but even then I had been forced to leave my job and join the police force, moving thirty miles from my home.

I sat on the edge of the bed and let out a big sigh. The sigh became a sob, and the sob became tears. The bedroom door flew open and both Annabel and Elvis bounded in. Annabel put her arms around me and Elvis gave me wet, sloppy kisses.

'Was I that obvious?' I said to Annabel as I dried my eyes on the handkerchief she had brought me.

'Hmm, it was clear the tears were going to fall eventually. We were listening out, weren't we, Elvis?'

'I was so sure, last night in London,' I said. 'But now, back in Stony End, I don't know. I really don't know. I wish I'd never gone, Annabel.'

The telephone in the hall began to ring. Annabel went to answer it, and then called me a few seconds later. 'Leo,' she mouthed as I came down the stairs.

I took a few seconds to compose myself. I did not want him to know I had been crying. 'Hello? Leo? Is anything wrong?'

'I'm such an idiot. I meant to say something very important,' he said.

'But the stupid ticket collector got in the way.'

'Oh . . . What was it?'

'I meant to tell you that I love you.'

7

If I could have stopped the world at that moment, I would have done. He loved me! To this day I can't actually remember if I said it back, though Annabel, who was standing nearby, said that I stammered something like '*I wov oo doo*', but as I'd started to cry again, she could not be completely sure.

He loved me and suddenly the prejudices of a few narrow-minded people in Stony End did not matter anymore.

So when I went back to the station the next morning, I was able to ignore the women who came into reception just so they could snub me. I was able to laugh off Mrs Higgins and Greta Norris, who both called in with cakes and deeply sympathetic looks. I even put up with the ribald comments of my fellow male officers in the tea room.

By the afternoon I noticed a sea change. The women who had come in to snub me earlier came in and smiled at me, asking how I was. Mrs Higgins and Greta Norris, whilst not asking for their cakes back — thank goodness! — both popped their heads around the door and gave me a thumbs-up. Even my fellow male officers were a little more respectful.

As I had work to do, I did not ask why things had changed. I completed my shift on the desk. Then, after shop closing time, and just as the ladies who inhabited the town hall steps were beginning their shifts, I went over there to speak to them.

'Hello, Pearl,' I said, finding the lady in question. She was talking to a man whom I did not recognise. I guessed he was a trucker who had stopped in Stony End for the night. When he saw me, he did a double take and then rushed off as if he had remembered another appointment.

'Well, thank you very much,' said Pearl.

'You're welcome,' I said sweetly. 'He looked the type to take off without paying anyway.'

Pearl rolled her eyes, making her drawn-on eyebrows almost disappear into her hairline, and then grinned.

It was fair to say we had a good relationship with the ladies on the town hall steps. Sometimes we arrested them, just to remind them that the law was the law, but mostly we turned a blind eye. More often than not the women were self-regulating. Pearl made sure that under-age girls were not welcomed in that community, and she also ensured that those who were old enough were not badly treated by the clientele. I don't say that I approved of their profession, but that did not mean I did not like them individually.

'What can I do for you, WPC Blandford?'

'I wanted to talk to you about Betty Norris. Alf told me that she . . . worked . . . with you just before her death.'

'Betty Norris?' Pearl frowned, and

her high eyebrows resembled a road sign for a hairpin bend. 'Betty Norris . . . '

'She was murdered in nineteen thirty-nine,' I explained. 'Just before the war. She and Ruth Yates. Both were strangled.'

'Oh, you mean Queenie.'

'Queenie?'

'She didn't use the name Betty here. Everyone called her Queenie. Because her name was Elizabeth. After Elizabeth the First, of course, not the current queen.'

'What did you know about her, Pearl? Was there a particular man that she hung around with?'

'We don't allow pimps around here, and we may have regular customers, but they're not allowed to monopolise the girls. It's always been the same. They start wanting favours and free goes otherwise.'

'What about a man she might have dated outside of this job?'

'Queenie didn't have much to do with men outside of her work on the steps,' said Pearl. 'I got the impression she didn't like them very much. Oh she did have a big row once, with a man who turned up to see her. Said he was her cousin.'

'Alf, you mean? Alf Norris.'

Pearl had to think about that. 'Now I come to think of it, it might have been, Alf. He wasn't on the beat then, and by the time he did come here, I'd forgotten about him seeing Queenie.'

'What was the argument about?'

'What is it always about when a male relative turns up? He wanted her to give up the job. They had a right row about it. Got a bit violent.'

'Who? Alf did?' I could hardly believe it.

'No. No, not him. Her. She slapped his face and told him to get lost. She told him she was a lost cause and not to come back ever again. I felt a bit sorry for him, really. He meant well. How could I have forgotten that was Alf? I suppose the war did it. That, and you see lots of men in this job. Their faces all mix together after a while. Hang on a minute. Let me get Tilly. She and Queenie often worked together.'

I did not want to ask exactly what that entailed. I just waited until Tilly, a woman who was even older and more weatherworn than Pearl, had finished talking to a man on the steps. Clearly they knew of my presence so any deal they made was going to happen later.

'Pearl said you wanted to know about Queenie?'

'That's right. Betty Norris.'

'What do you want to know?'

'I wondered if there were any men in her life. I know about her cousin.'

'Yeah, Pearl tells me that was Alf Norris. We didn't realise at the time. Mind you, I think Greta had fed him up a bit more by the time he came to work at the station. Her cousin, as I remember him, was a scrawny little thing.'

'What about other men, Tilly? Do you know who she went off with on the night she died?'

'Why bring this up, all these years later?'

'Because we think her death may be linked with the woman who was found in the castle grounds. Please, Tilly, anything you can tell us . . . '

'There'd been a man sniffing around who seemed to take to Queenie. What was his name — ? Clarence something. No, George Clarence. That was it. He was an airman. Big talker. Flown this, that and the other on secret missions. To be honest, when men are paying, we don't care what rubbish they spout. He said he was from South America originally. He took a shine to Queenie, and she seemed to like him. Well, she said she liked the idea of moving away and starting another life. She didn't get the chance.' Tilly's eyes looked damp.

'You were really close to her, weren't you?'

'We'd both been messed around,' was all Tilly would say.

'Did you see George Clarence after she died?'

'No, I can't say I did. But the war started not long after, and no one stayed in one place very long for a good while. Servicemen came and went, and he was just another one.'

'Could you describe him?'

'Ooh, duck, no. Not this long after.'

'If you remember anything, Tilly, will you call me at the station?'

'If I remember, yes.'

'Oh, one other thing. The Paisley scarf that Betty — Queenie — was strangled with. Did she wear it a lot?'

'I can't say I remember,' said Tilly. 'No, I don't think so. In fact, I can't say if I saw her in it at all. But that means nothing. She could have bought it that day.'

'Yes, I suppose she could have.'

I did not think that she had. I was fast coming to the conclusion that the man — Harold or Arthur York or George Clarence — had brought the scarf with him. Perhaps as a gift. Or perhaps as a premeditated means of strangling the women. I shuddered at the thought.

As I rode home on my Vespa, Stony End looked like the most innocent place on earth, yet darkness lay at its core. I began to blame myself less for taking my happiness where I could find it. Why not enjoy stolen moments with Leo when so many awful things happened in the world?

When I arrived home I found Annabel in the kitchen, making cheese on toast. 'Do you want some, sweetie?' She had a strange, knowing grin on her face.

'Oh yes, please. What's made you smile?'

'Leo.'

'Oh . . . ' I was not sure I liked that idea. Annabel was stunningly beautiful and, as fellow doctors, she and Leo had more in common than he and I did.

'No, not in that way,' she said, waving her hand dismissively. 'I was on the ward this afternoon during visiting time when Leo came in to see Alf Norris.'

'Oh, how is Alf?' I had completely forgotten about Alf's operation. I had even forgotten to ask Greta how he was. I had not been a very good friend whilst engrossed in my own problems.

'He's fine, fine. The operation was a success and he's going home tomorrow. Anyway, that's not it. One of the consultants was there. Mr Jameson. Do you know him?'

I shook my head. 'I can't say I do.'

'He's an utter pig. Anyway, he was teasing Leo about your weekend away. Bear in mind, it was visiting time and loads of people from Stony End were there, including Greta Norris. 'How was she, old man?' Jameson asked him. Leo shrugged and said, 'No idea, mate. She kept her door locked all weekend.'' Annabel laughed. 'You could see the women breaking their necks to end visiting time and get back to town to tell what they knew. And Greta said to me, 'We should have trusted our girl.' Well, of course I didn't let the cat out of the bag, but it was all I could do not to laugh. Leo winked at me as he went past. He must know you'd tell me the truth.'

'I think I *wov* him more than ever,' I sighed happily.

8

I rode the Vespa up to the nursing home to see Mrs Atkins and discuss her missing bicycle. I felt I had been neglecting her, so it was time to bring her up to date with what we knew.

Not that there was much to tell. Few people remembered the night a bike went missing over twenty-one years before. Even Mrs Atkins was not sure on what night it had happened, though my dad's notes said it was Friday the nineteenth of May, some months before the war started. Mrs Atkins had been attending the birth of a baby boy. She had left her bicycle outside the house whilst she went inside.

'It was a long and difficult labour,' Mrs Atkins had told me. 'I was there till dawn. When I came out, my bicycle was gone.'

According to my father's notes, few

people saw anything on account of there being a new moon that night. Plus people in Stony End tended to go to bed early and get up early, to make the most of the light.

The war had been some months away. Germany would invade Poland on the first of September. But there was activity in Britain in preparation for a war. Young men and women were already signing up for the forces. There had been an RAF training camp not far from Stony End, and some of the young men used to come down from the camp for a drink in the Cunning Woman.

I suspected that the theft of the bicycle had been a prank by one of them. It occurred to me that if I could find one of those men — assuming they had survived the war — he might be able to answer the mystery for me. It was unlikely anyone would be charged so long after the event, particularly if it was a prank.

All this I explained to Mrs Atkins when I visited her.

'Thank you, WPC Blandford. I think you're probably right. It was just a prank. I'm really wasting your time, aren't I?'

'Not at all,' I said. It was only half a lie. With a repeated murderer on the loose our resources were few, but I did not want to put aside the more trivial cases. Finding out what happened to her bicycle was important to Mrs Atkins. So it was important to me. 'Mrs Atkins, did you know any of the airmen based at the camp?'

'Oh, let me see . . . ' She stared into space and for a moment I thought I'd lost her. 'There was young Norman Rodgers. Mrs Rodgers's eldest. Clever boy, he was. He was based there.'

'Is he still alive?'

'Yes, yes he is. But he was badly burned when his plane came down in . . . oh where was it? Somewhere in Germany. Then they took him to a prisoner of war camp, where I don't think he was treated terribly well. He's a bit of a recluse now. His young wife couldn't cope with the way he looked, so she took the children to live with her parents in Derby. He lives on the Springfield Estate in one of the prefabs, near to . . . oh who is it?'

'Greta and Alf Norris?'

'Yes, that's right.'

'I'll go and talk to him then. Maybe he remembers something happening that night.'

After a cup of tea and a chat with Mrs Atkins, I left her and made my way back towards the town. I was not sure about calling on Norman Rodgers unannounced, but I did not know when I might have time to ask him again. The sarge was already complaining about me wasting time on Mrs Atkins's bicycle.

I parked my Vespa on the road outside and tentatively went to knock on the door. The garden was rather unkempt and the windows were covered over with yellowing newspapers. I had passed this house dozens of times whilst on the beat or visiting Alf and

116

Greta, and for some reason I had thought it was unoccupied. It showed that whilst I might have thought I knew everyone in Stony End, there were still a few people who, for reasons of their own, kept out of our way. If they had not been arrested, or called us for help, then it would be quite easy for us to go years without dealing with them.

I was about to knock again when I heard shuffling from inside. 'What is it? What do you want?' a gruff voice called through the door. 'I'm not buying anything.'

'Mr Rodgers, this is WPC Blandford from the station. I wonder if I might have a word with you.'

The door opened a little, to show a dusty, dark hallway and half a man's face. From that half I could see he was not much over forty. Many of the airmen who flew in the war had been ridiculously young and I reminded myself that Wing Commander Guy Gibson, who flew in the Dambusters operation, had only been twenty-six when he died. 'Come about the kids throwing stones at last, have you? It's about time. Alf said he was going to do something.'

'Alf has been in hospital having his ingrown toenail done, so he sent me instead.' It was a lie, but I felt it was probably my only way into the house. If I said I had come to talk about a missing bicycle from over twenty years ago, he would probably shut the door in my face. 'May I come in?'

It never occurred to me back then that it might be dangerous to go into a man's house alone. It was a different world where we trusted each other. Yes, bad things happened, but we did not go out every day assuming that they would. When awful events occurred they were a surprise and not something we expected with every waking breath.

'You might want to cover your eyes, lass,' he said. He opened the door a little wider. I wish I could say that his appearance did not bother me. I wish I could say I took it all in my stride. But

Mrs Atkins had been right. Norman Rodgers had been very badly burned, and I was not prepared for what I saw. I think I managed to compose myself, but my heart hammered as I entered the house.

Why I should be afraid, I don't know. But then, as now, we tend to associate goodness with beauty and evil with ugliness. I reminded myself that this was a man who had fought in the war, and his injuries had been a result of him committing very brave deeds.

'Well, you've stayed longer than my wife did after I arrived home from the war, so you're not doing bad, lass,' he said with a trace of bitterness in his voice. He led me into the sitting room. 'I shouldn't be too hard on her. I was a good-looking lad in my day.' He went to the mantelpiece and took down a picture, handing it to me. 'She didn't expect to spend her life with this.' He pointed to his scar-puckered face.

It was a wedding picture. He had indeed been a handsome young man and his wife very pretty. She looked very proud to be by his side, and I wondered how important his looks had been to her. How much did she love him for himself, and how much because other girls must have wanted him too?

Next to the picture was a medal, presumably that Mr Rodgers had won for his bravery, and next to that another photograph of him standing next to a plane. Why could his wife not have been proud of that? Then guilt overtook me. I did not know if I could be as brave if Leo ever altered beyond recognition, so I was in no position to judge this girl who had gone into her marriage seeing nothing but sunshine and rainbows and a gloriously handsome young husband.

'I'm sorry,' I said, though it seemed the wrong thing to say.

'Why? You didn't do anything.'

The room was surprisingly neat and tidy, decorated with a grey G-Plan suite and a matching table under the window. I got the impression that the room was seldom used and wondered where Mr Rodgers spent most of his time if not here. 'So,' I said, becoming professional. One thing about being a policewoman is that you can hide behind the uniform. It may not have covered my face, but it was as good as any mask. 'Tell me about the problems you've been having.' I took out my notebook.

'Oh, the usual stuff. Teenage kids hanging around. Those Teddy Boys. No, they're not Teddy Boys now, are they? They're Mods and Rockers. I can't tell the difference between them. They throw stuff at the house. Call me 'Quasimodo'.'

'How long has this been going on?' I was horrified. What a dreadful way to treat a man who had been a hero to his country.

'A couple of months. I know Alf had a quiet word with some of them and it stopped for a while. But . . . well it's my fault, I suppose. I react when they do come around. I try to ignore it, but . . . if I've had a few drinks, which happens often, I run out yelling at them. I don't bother anyone around here. My sister does my shopping for me, and any other errands, so I don't upset the ladies in the butchers' queue. I never go out of this house, yet these kids . . . they won't leave me alone. I just want a quiet life, lass.'

'I can understand that. I'll put in a report to the sarge and see if we can't get extra beat bobbies out here. Do you know who any of these lads are?'

'Yeah, I know one of them. He's the son . . . no, not son . . . brother . . . of Doctor Stanhope.'

'Joe Garland, you mean?' Joe was Leo's half-brother, and when Joe's mother was committed to an asylum in my first year at Stony End, Leo had taken over Joe's care. 'I can't believe it.'

'I'm not making it up!'

'No, no, of course not. It's just not like Joe.'

'Well, to be fair, I only saw him for the first time last night. He'd not been amongst the troublemakers before. But

I know him because he sometimes came down with Doctor Stanhope when I needed treatment. He didn't come in. He'd just hang about outside.'

'I'll have a word with Leo . . . I mean, Doctor Stanhope. I'm sure we can impress on Joe that what he's doing is wrong. He's usually a good lad. Is there anything else you'd like to tell me?'

'No, that's about it.'

I made my way towards the door. 'Well, thank you. Actually . . . ' I paused, pretending it was something that had only just occurred to me. 'I was talking to Mrs Atkins. Nurse Atkins?'

'Oh yeah, I remember her. Nice lady, she was, when I was recuperating.'

'It was about her missing bicycle. It was years ago, before the war, and we think that some lads from the airfield might have taken it as a prank. Do you remember anything like that happening?'

To my surprise, Norman Rodgers laughed. 'Was that her bike?'

'You know about it?'

'It was one of the lads. He'd had a few too many to drink and almost missed the curfew, so he took the bike and rode it back to the airfield. I think we stripped it for parts.'

'Oh well. That's something I can tell Mrs Atkins, I suppose.'

'Yeah, the daft fool. Always up to some prank, was Harold York.'

9

'Harold York?' I spun around to face Mr Rodgers. His scars no longer concerned me. 'You knew Harold York?'

'Yeah, of course I did. We were billeted together at the airfield. He'd come from — oh where was it? South Africa. No, South America. That was it. He was a complete madman and not always very honest. They once court-martialled him for flying a plane under a bridge. Well, it was all just a show really. To be honest, the top brass liked us doing these things, to help train us. But they couldn't sanction it. Danger to the public and all that. I once landed mine in the middle of the Great North Road. It was all about pushing it to see how far we could go. Harold liked to push it a bit more than most.'

'Were you aware that Harold York

was involved with a woman called Ruth Yates?'

'Ruth Yates? Hang on a minute. Wasn't she an artist or something? She died here in Stony End, didn't she?' I nodded. 'I remember her, I think,' said Mr Rodgers. 'We met her in the Cunning Woman when she was visiting Stony End. She was a really good-looking woman. She had red hair, just like yours. Sometimes it felt like she was only chatting us up so we'd buy her drinks. But I think she really liked Harold. He was handsome and had loads of tall tales to tell. Most of them rubbish, if you ask me. He reckoned he was a great polo player in South America. Then some adventure to find the source of the Amazon. Or was it the Nile? Yes, it was the Nile. Well every schoolboy knows the story of Livingstone and Stanley, so that didn't wash with me, but I think Ruth just liked to pretend to believe him. He was good-looking and bought her drinks, so she wasn't likely to argue.'

'What happened to York? Is he still in Stony End?'

Mr Rodgers shook his head. 'No, he went back to South America, I think. He had a wife over there. He was thrown out of the RAF, despite the war. He'd cashed a couple of dodgy cheques, and then he stole stuff from the lockers. Well, none of us were squeaky clean. I'd been in borstal for a bit before joining up. But you don't steal off your own, you know.'

'What about George Clarence? Did you know a man of that name?'

'That was one of the names Harold used when signing forged cheques.'

'He's the same man?'

'Why are you suddenly interested in Harold York?'

'I don't know if you know, but Ruth Yates was murdered.'

'Yeah, I know. It was the night that Harold came back on the bicycle. He would never forgive himself for leaving her.'

I stopped for a moment, wanting to

kick myself. Why had I not noticed the corresponding dates? But why should I? As far as I knew they had been two totally unconnected events, happening in some non-specific time before the war. It had not occurred to me to connect them. No doubt other crimes had taken place in Stony End around the same time.

'Then another woman, Betty Norris, was murdered. Erm . . . she was also known as Queenie.'

'Oh, Queenie. Yeah, we knew about her. I didn't bother with Pearl and her lot. I had a girl. But some of the lads went there. They weren't allowed in the pub. The girls on the town hall steps, I mean. So it took a special trip to see them.'

'She befriended a man called George Clarence. Then she died.'

'You're not saying that Harold York was involved, are you?'

'I don't know, Mr Rodgers. But it's possible that Harold murdered her then stole Nurse Atkins's bicycle to make a getaway.'

'On a bicycle?' He grinned, and it completely altered his features. For a moment, I saw the boy he had been all those years ago.

'I know of someone who made a getaway on a brewery dray. A bicycle would be quicker.'

'No, come on. Harold might have been a bit of a shyster, but he was no murderer.'

'Are you sure about that? Are you sure that he wasn't capable of violence?'

Norman Rodgers sat down on the wood-framed G-Plan sofa and put his head in his hands. I suspected it was the first time he had sat there in a long time. 'He could get violent when he'd had a drink, yeah, but that was with other men. You just don't treat women like that.'

'Mr Rodgers, do you know anything about a Paisley scarf?'

His head shot up. 'What about it?'

'Both women were strangled with such a scarf. What do you know?'

'I'd bought one for my mother. It was

in my locker but someone stole it.' He looked up, his eyes narrowing. 'It was stolen, honestly. I didn't connect it with Harold though, as he normally just took money or stuff he could sell, like watches and cigarette cases.'

'I may need you to come to the station and make a statement to that effect.'

'I'm not going out. I haven't been through that door in years. If you want a statement, you'll have to come here and get it.'

'Very well,' I said. 'We'll do that.'

I rushed back to the station to tell the sarge everything I had found out.

'All we need do,' I said excitedly when I had explained, 'is to find out where Harold York is. If he's been in trouble with the police, there will be a record.'

The sarge nodded. 'Good work, Blandford. And all because of a bicycle. I'd never have thought of that.'

'I think that Mrs Atkins did,' I said. 'Not consciously, but something made her fret over that bicycle. I wonder what brought it on.'

10

I felt sure that as soon as we caught up with Harold York alias George Clarence, the case would be closed. There was the issue of one of the scarves possibly belonging to Mr Rodgers. What if he had only said it was stolen? It would be handy, if he was the killer, to pin it on some man who was probably living somewhere in South America, using yet another assumed name.

I wondered if Rodgers had been seeing one of the women and gave it to her as a gift, then strangled her with it because she had threatened to tell his girlfriend. That might make sense with Ruth Yates, who appeared to have been looking for the love of her life; but Betty Norris had been a prostitute, and they treated their clients as a priest treated his parishioners, with all dealings being as sacred as the confessional.

In the meantime, I decided to call up to Leo's and have a word with his brother, Joe. Leo lived at Stanhope Manor, a glorious Georgian house that stood on a hill overlooking Stony End. There was a strange car in the driveway. It was huge, with big wings. It took me a moment to realise it was a Cadillac, because I was too busy wondering why it was there. I had never seen it before. Leo's sister, Julia, had gone to America, and I wondered if she had returned.

Leo opened the door before I had dismounted from the Vespa. His face was grave and serious.

'I'm sorry, Leo,' I said. 'But I need to talk to you about Joe. There's been an allegation made against him. I haven't reported it yet. I thought we could deal with it together.'

'Bobbie,' was all he replied, hoarsely. 'I was going to come and speak to you.'

'Oh, do you know about it? Did he tell you? Well that's a start. I don't know what made him do such a thing. He's normally a good lad.'

At that moment, Joe followed Leo out of the house. 'Is it about Mr Rodgers?' he asked. Aged sixteen, he already had his elder brother's good looks. The sixties had not yet found its own style, as in the mop-top haircut popularised by the Beatles a couple of years later, so Joe's hair was swept back at the sides with the fringe curled over into a quiff, like a Teddy Boy. He wore a short-sleeved white shirt, black jacket and black drainpipe trousers. Already over six feet tall, he showed every sign of being a real heartbreaker in the future.

'Yes, Joe, I'm afraid it is.' I tried to sound official, but it was difficult with a boy I knew and liked. 'Whatever possessed you?'

'I was upset, that's all.' Joe looked at Leo then down at the ground. 'I went for a walk and saw the boys, and decided to join in. Just to let off steam. That's all. I didn't mean to . . . ' He looked at Leo again and for the first time I wondered what was going on.

'Leo, don't you have anything to say

to Joe about this?'

'Things have been a little difficult here,' said Leo. He was staring at me in a way I could not fathom.

'Joe, will you come with me, please?' I asked. Joe was about to refuse, but Leo pushed him forward, not unkindly. 'You're not under arrest,' I assured him. 'I just want to introduce you to someone.'

'Go on, Joe, go with her. Take your medicine like a man.'

'As if you'd know about that,' said Joe, bitterly.

'I'll see you later,' I said to Leo, smiling. He did not smile back, but with Joe there I did not want to ask what was wrong. No doubt he would tell me. I had not seen him much since our mutual declaration of love over the phone, but with us both so busy with our careers that was not unusual.

'Is Julia back?' I called over my shoulder to Joe, who was riding pillion on the Vespa.

'No.'

'I was just going by the American car.' I slowed down a little so I could hear his reply.

'I'm not to say anything until Leo has spoken to you. Only . . . I'm really sorry, Bobbie. About Mr Rodgers and everything.'

I drove the Vespa into the Springfield Estate and for the second time that day parked outside Mr Rodgers's home. 'Come on,' I told Joe, getting off the bike.

It took Mr Rodgers a minute or two to open the door, and I guessed that on seeing Joe walk up the path, he had hesitated about whether to let us in.

'Mr Rodgers, thank you for answering the door. This is Joe Garland.'

'I know that,' said Mr Rodgers. He opened the door wider, to show all his fire-damaged face. 'Hello.' I heard Joe's sharp intake of breath, but to his credit, he did not show too much horror.

'Joe, this is Mr Rodgers. Joe, say hello.'

'Hello.'

'May we come in, Mr Rodgers? It will only take a minute or two.'

'Come on then.'

Once again he led me into the neat sitting room, but this time the door to the kitchen was open, and I saw a small Formica table near to the back door with a seat pulled out. On the table were books, cigarettes, an ashtray and a half-empty cup of tea. It answered the question of where Mr Rodgers spent all his time. I walked through the door and looked out at the garden. It was unkempt, like the front garden, but with signs of him having tried. A high fence surrounded the garden, hiding him from the neighbours.

'It gets too much for me,' he said, by way of explanation.

'Joe, did you know that Mr Rodgers flew bombers during the war?'

Joe shook his head, but he was already looking towards the pictures and the medal on the fireplace.

'Mr Rodgers is on his own now and his bravery has been forgotten by stupid boys who don't appreciate that the freedom they enjoy is because of men like him.'

'What sort of plane was it?' asked Joe, his eyes locked on that one picture. 'Sir,' he added for good measure.

'A Hawker Typhoon.'

'That's a single-engine, single-seater plane, isn't it, sir?'

'That's right, lad, and it was nearly written off, until we found out it was the only one capable of catching the Focke-Wulf.'

'That must have been fantastic. And frightening.'

With neither realising, they moved closer together to look at the picture, and I sensed them begin to relax in each other's presence.

'It was both.'

'I don't understand, sir. If you did all this, why are you afraid of us lads? You could probably see us off without any problems.'

'I didn't fight the war and get this — ' He pointed to his face. ' — so that I could bully kids half my age. Besides, I'm more afraid now than I ever was during the war. I'm old before my time, I'm alone, and I don't see a friendly face from one day to the next. That has a way of making a man afraid of his own shadow, let alone a bunch of healthy young lads who could probably kick me from here to kingdom come. You forget how to be with people. How to hold your head up high. How to fight for your rights.'

'I'm sorry, sir,' said Joe. 'I truly am sorry. I was only doing it because . . . ' He looked at me. 'Because of things I can't talk about yet. But I shouldn't have taken it out on you. If there's any way I can make it up to you . . . '

'If Mr Rodgers agrees, perhaps you could help him in his garden,' I suggested. 'Once a week, just till you go back to school in September. You can start by cleaning up the mess you and the other lads left in the front garden. What do you say, Mr Rodgers?'

'I'll pay you,' Mr Rodgers said to Joe.

'No,' I protested. 'The idea is for Joe to learn his lesson.'

'And the lesson he'd learn is that it's all right to be used as slave labour,' said Mr Rodgers. 'That's one of the things I fought against. So what do you say, lad? Want to earn a bit of spending money?'

'I'm not short of money,' said Joe, 'because my brother sees me right. But yeah, I'll do it. Perhaps, if you don't mind, you can tell me more about the war. Leo was too young to serve in it, and I wasn't born till nearly the end.'

'We've got a deal, lad. Thank you, WPC Blandford.' Mr Rodgers smiled and it transformed his face again. It seemed to me that he had nothing to worry about when going out, but that was a mountain to help him climb on another day.

Joe and I left him to his own devices, with Joe promising to return at ten o'clock the next morning. 'He's a nice bloke,' said Joe, when we went back to the Vespa. I handed him his helmet and started to put my own on.

'Yes, he is.'

'Not a monster, like the others thought.'

'Real monsters seldom look like monsters,' I said, thinking of the handsome young man who had probably killed Ruth, Betty and the unnamed woman in the castle grounds. 'Come on, I'll take you home.'

'I don't want to go home, Bobbie.'

'What's happened, Joe? It can't just be about Mr Rodgers. Have you and Leo had a fight? Is it because Julia has come back and your mum hasn't?'

'It's not Julia and it's not my mum,' said Joe. 'I'm so angry with him, Bobbie, because I like you. I think you're brilliant, even though you're just a girl.'

I grinned. 'Well, thank you for that.'

'I'm not supposed to say anything. He wants to break it to you himself. But he's just a liar and a cheat, Bobbie, and I don't know why we ever trusted him. She's not even nice. She's horrid.'

'She?' I said, feeling my blood run cold.

Before Joe could answer, I heard a car behind us and turned to see Leo pull up at the curb. The red sports car had been involved in our first meeting when, having chased after Annabel's runaway car, I had managed to crash straight into Leo. For me it had been love at first sight, though it took me a while to realise that.

'I'll walk back,' said Joe, handing me his helmet. 'Please don't be mad at me for not telling you, Bobbie.' He clambered off, his long gangly legs almost tripping him up.

'Not telling me what?' I called after him, but he was already at the end of the street and whether he heard me or pretended not to, I don't know.

'Bobbie, leave the Vespa here for a while,' said Leo, standing next to his car door. 'Come for a drive with me. We'll go to the pub.'

Without speaking, but with a strong sense of foreboding, I took off my helmet and, along with Joe's, locked it in the back box of the Vespa.

Though we were both quiet on the way to the pub, I could feel the tension every time Leo glanced across to look at me. My stomach knotted and I began to rehearse all the things I would say to him to show myself as a sophisticated modern woman.

'Yes, Leo, you're right. Two people who can't agree on whether Buddy Holly or Elvis Presley was the King of Rock 'n' Roll should not be together.'

'Yes, Leo, I understand that you've decided to give up medicine and go and live in a monastery.'

Not that I had heard of any orders of monks who drove American Cadillacs. That car remained imprinted on my brain and I knew that it was the key to what was going on with Leo. But my mind also refused to accept the possibility of there being another woman. Either I was naïve or stupid, but it seemed to me that with Stony End being such a small place, I would have heard sooner or later. Greta and Mrs Higgins would have told me, even if everyone else just whispered amongst themselves. Certainly someone driving around Stony End in a Cadillac would have been noticed.

We reached the pub and I followed Leo in, realising I was still in uniform. But I was off duty so I accepted his offer of a gin and tonic. Brian Lancaster waved at me from behind the bar and then went back to flirting with some of the ladies who had called in from the bank. I noticed that young Verity was amongst them. Verity had been a homeless teenager when I first met her, but she had sorted herself out to find a good position at the bank. She was dressed smartly in a blue suit, with her hair curled perfectly around her pretty face. I smiled over at her and wondered if she would have a word with Joe too. He might listen to someone near to his own age. I decided to have a word with her.

Life, I thought, was normal, despite my fears about Leo, and I would continue to treat it as normal until told otherwise. That included sorting out Joe, just in case meeting Mr Rodgers had not quite curbed him of his sudden wildness.

'I've arranged for Joe to do some gardening for Mr Rodgers,' I said when Leo came back with the drinks.

'Good, good. It'll do him good.'

'Good,' I said, already sick of the word. 'I think Mr Rodgers can teach Joe a lot about the war and the air force. So, are you going to tell me why you and Joe have fallen out? Don't tell me, he bought that Cadillac with his pocket money and you're jealous that you didn't think of it first.'

Leo looked down at his drink and to my surprise, drank it all down in one go. 'I think I'll get another,' he said. 'How about you?'

'How about you don't, because you're driving,' I said, assuming my professional air.

'Yes, officer,' he said, seeming annoyed with me.

'All right,' I sighed. 'Tell me what it's all about? If it's over between us, Leo, for goodness sake just say so. I can't bear this much longer.'

'It's not over. At least my feelings for you will never end, Bobbie. I just have something to tell you.'

'What? Some dark secret from your past again?' To my horror, his expression told me that I had hit the nail squarely on the head. 'What?' I said. 'Tell me!'

'When I was in medical school, some friends and I took a trip to America during the summer holidays. We worked our way up the west coast, then across to Las Vegas. I got a job as a croupier in a casino. I met a girl. Cindy-Lou. She was a dancer at the same casino.'

'And you were in love with her. You still are.'

'No! Definitely not. Oh it was a mad holiday, Bobbie. I wish I could explain it to you, but Las Vegas seems as if it's set apart from the rest of the world. It's unreal. I had not quite got over my wild streak. I was drinking heavily, because it's what my friends were doing and I was stupid. Do you know you can get married in Las Vegas without going through all the rigmarole of having the banns read? You can just walk into a church and walk out five minutes later as a married couple.'

'No. No, I didn't know that.' An icy finger ran down my spine, causing me to shiver despite the bright summer's day.

'Marriage there is a big business.'

'I see.' At least I thought I was beginning to see, but I wanted him to say it. I refused on principle to help him tell me the truth.

'So one night I got very drunk and . . . I woke up the next morning with Cindy-Lou at my side. She told me that we had married and had the licence to prove it. But we both agreed it was ridiculous and a result of too much drink. We agreed to an annulment on grounds of non-consummation, reasoning we were too drunk for it to be otherwise. I gave her some money to go and file the necessary paperwork and that was the last I saw of her. As far as I was concerned, it was all over.'

'But now . . . '

'She turned up yesterday morning, telling me that the marriage was never annulled and that we are still married.'

I began to understand how Anthony Newley felt. I wanted the world to stop there and then, and not to hear any more of what Leo told me. But life went on around me. The women from the bank were laughing in the corner as Brian told them some tall tale. The old soaks who propped up the bar on a daily basis were talking about how Kennedy had nearly brought about the end of the world. I wanted to tell them that he had not, because the world was ending there and then for me.

'You, erm . . . you don't want to divorce her then?' Had Leo been married to a woman for many years and had lived with her, I would never have suggested such a thing. I believed, and still do believe, in the sanctity of marriage. But this was a woman he had only known briefly. She was also part of

147

a big secret he had, once again, failed to tell me, but at the time I was not thinking about that aspect. I had just been hit with news that rendered me incapable of rational thought.

'I would. I would divorce her like a shot if it were that simple. But we had made one major mistake, Bobbie.'

I think I knew what it was before he told me, but still I waited, as the world resolutely insisted on turning, despite all my mental efforts to slip into suspended animation.

'Tell me,' I said hoarsely. I closed my eyes, waiting for the final curtain to fall on our love.

'For some reason she decided to wait, rather than have the marriage annulled. Two months later, she found out that we did consummate our marriage after all. Bobbie . . . I'm so sorry, but I found out last night that not only am I still married, but I also have a ten-year-old son.'

11

The world not only stopped, it cracked and fell apart, collapsing into billions of tiny pieces around me. I might have been able to fight against an ill-advised marriage. But a child was a different matter. A child was innocent and had not asked for the circumstances of his conception.

'I have to try for his sake,' said Leo.

I nodded dumbly. 'I know. What . . . where is he? Up at the house?'

Leo shook his head. 'He's with Cindy-Lou's family in America. She didn't want to bring him over until she had spoken to me. I wired some money across yesterday so he should be over soon. I can't wait to meet him and . . .' As if realising his enthusiasm was out of place, he fell into silence.

'What's his name?' I don't know why I was even asking. I didn't want to know. Knowing made things real. I should have got up and walked out, but I seemed to have become glued to my seat. I could not cry. I could not scream and yell. It had all happened before he met me. But a nagging voice at the back of my head reminded me that it was just one more of Leo's secrets. How many more would there be? Not that it mattered anymore. Any more mysteries surrounding him would be Cindy-Lou's problem now, not mine.

'Michael, but they call him Mikey.'

'I need to go.' I snatched up my bag.

'Bobbie, it changes nothing about my feelings for you.'

'Then it should, because I've made that mistake once and I'm not doing it again. Not even for you, Leo, and I love you more than I ever loved the Italian. You have a wife and child now. Go to them. Leave me be.'

I managed to stand up, but too quickly so that the room swam around me. He stood up and caught me, but his touch burned and reminded me too

150

much of how intimate we had been. With me he had used protection. That was something at least, but it also felt like another blow against me because with Cindy-Lou he had thrown caution to the wind. I should have been the one he lost all control with, not her.

I wandered around Stony End, putting off the moment I had to go back home and tell Annabel what had happened. I walked in the park, then past the chip shop. The aroma that would normally have had me rushing in to fill up on fish and chips made me feel nauseous.

It began to rain, and I had no overcoat or umbrella, but still I kept walking. I went up to the Springfield Estate, where Mr Rodgers stayed hidden behind his net curtains and Greta and Alf were no doubt sitting down to their evening meal. I picked up the Vespa and rode it all around the district as the rain poured down on me. I went up to the castle and around Little Stony. There was something I needed to do there. Someone I needed to talk to, which had got forgotten in all the confusion, but I could not remember who.

I headed for the Stockport road, past the transport caff where the town hall steps girls spent most of their days, then back along the lanes towards Stony End. I had a feeling I was being followed at some point, but when I looked back the car was too far away, and when I looked back again later it had gone. But I was sure it was a black Zephyr. Perhaps some colleague off on a case.

Annabel was waiting on the doorstep when I finally pulled up to our cottage.

'Oh my darling girl,' she said, holding out her arms. 'I've been so worried about you. I wanted to send out a search party, but the sarge said to give you time and that you'd come home.'

'He sent a car to follow me,' I said, shivering. 'I saw it.'

'I thought he might.'

'Leo . . . '

'It's all right, sweetie. I know. We all know now. Leo telephoned me. He was concerned about you.'

'He's married! With a child!' I screamed, forgetting I was still standing on the garden path in the rain, where all the neighbours could hear me. 'He has no right to be concerned about me. How could he, Annabel? How could he? He couldn't ask me to marry him, oh no! But he managed to marry some trollop he barely knew and have a child with her! I hate him. I hate him and the sooner I get away from here the better!'

I ran inside and picked up the phone, dialling my mother's number. 'Mum?'

Annabel followed me and picked up a bath towel that had been put in the chair in the hallway. She wrapped it around my shoulders and began gently rubbing my hair dry. I'm ashamed to say I swatted her off with a flick of my hand.

'Bobbie, sweetheart, what is it?' my mother asked.

'Mum, I want to come home.'

'Oh . . . well it's not possible at the moment, Bobbie. I . . . I don't have room now.'

'Mum, you have two bedrooms. I shan't get in the way of you and your boyfriend, if that's what you're worried about.'

'Bobbie, I don't quite like what you're implying.'

'Oh forget it!' I slammed the phone down and ran upstairs, closing my bedroom door with a resounding crash.

I heard the phone ring and Annabel calling me, but I ignored her. I did not want to speak to anyone. My mother, who should have been there for me in my darkest hour, had let me down, and all because of a man.

Sometime later, Annabel came in and put a cup of tea and a couple of Jaffa cakes on my bedside table. I managed to murmur 'thanks' but I was not ready to talk to her about Leo yet.

By the following morning I told myself I had recovered. No way would I spend my life crying over a man.

Especially one who treated marriage in such a cavalier fashion. I told myself I'd had a lucky escape.

I dressed in my clean uniform and went off to the station without having breakfast. It was my turn on the desk, so I checked the rota to see what everyone else was doing that day, so that I could contact them if necessary. We didn't yet have portable police radios, so the beat bobbies had particular contact points throughout Stony End, either public or police telephone boxes, where they had to be at certain times of day. If anything came in, I was to ring the box nearest to that part of their beat and keep ringing it until they replied.

Mrs Higgins came in as I was making a list of things to do. 'I don't want to talk about it,' I snapped at her, then immediately regretted it. 'Sorry.'

'Quite right too, but I thought you'd like some coconut cake for your elevenses. Your favourite.'

'Oh, thank you.'

'Why don't you come to tea tonight? It's only pork chops, but I know you like my onion gravy.'

'I'll see. I can't promise.' I knew she would want to find out more about what happened, and I was not ready to talk to anyone else yet.

Greta Norris was no more than five minutes behind her. 'Apple strudel,' she said. 'Your favourite.'

All right, so I may have misled them both as to my favourite cake. The thing with cake is that my favourite was usually whatever I was eating at the time.

'Why don't you come to tea with us tonight?' asked Greta. 'It's only stewing steak, but I know how much you love my Yorkshire pudding. I'll make an extra-big one.'

Even all these years later, I can still taste the food that Mrs Higgins and Greta used to make for me. Somehow nothing else has ever compared. My own mother had let me down, but they were there, ready to fill me up with food. It was their way of showing love. Their rivalry over who would be my surrogate mother could be cloying at times, but oh how I miss them now.

With a mumbled apology to Greta, I had to get on with my work. I would have to let both ladies down so as not to offend the other. Besides, I owed Annabel some time. She had been there waiting for me when I returned home. She had brought me tea and Jaffa cakes. I owed my friend a few hours. I decided to cook a meal for her. Annabel worked such long hours at the hospital and more often than not, we existed on baked beans on toast. But not tonight. I decided to cook sausages and mash, and try making some of Mrs Higgins's onion gravy. Maybe I'd do a Yorkshire pudding too. In Stony End there were no silly rules about having to have Yorkshire puddings with beef.

Thinking of the lovely meal I would cook — unfortunately in those days my imagination rather outweighed my cooking abilities — helped to take my mind off things. For the first hour or so on the desk, I was on pretty good form.

Then at around eleven o'clock a woman walked in. She was very well-dressed in a smart blue suit and black high heels, with a pillar-box hat. Her hair was the colour of corn on a summer morning but I suspected it was not natural. 'Oh hi,' she said. 'I appear to have gotten myself lost.' She looked me up and down and appeared to find me wanting. She was American and immediately I knew who she was and why she had wandered into the police station.

'What are you looking for, madam?' I asked, with icy politeness.

'The post office.'

'It's the building opposite,' I said with a tight smile. I added waspishly, 'The one that says 'post office' in big red letters.'

'Why, thank you.' She smiled an equally tight smile back at me and left.

So that was Cindy-Lou Stanhope. How could I ever compete? She was polished and beautiful. What was more, she had the one thing I would never have. Sex appeal. And she had it in droves. I felt frumpy and fat. Norman Hartnell had not shown interest in the attire of policewomen yet, so my blue serge uniform often resembled a coal sack.

I did not do so well after that. Every phone call felt trivial and every person who called in seemed to just be wasting my time. One call was the last straw.

'Look, you little oik,' I snapped into the phone, 'little boys like you who are fascinated by the colour of women's knickers usually grow up to be rapists and murderers.'

'Blandford!'

'Sarge!' I was so shocked to realise he was behind me, I dropped the phone.

'In my office now, please.'

I duly followed him in, leaving one of my colleagues to man the desk. 'Sorry, Sarge, but the little . . . idiot . . . has been phoning all morning.'

'Yes, and he's probably about ten

years old, what with the kids being off school. Perhaps he's a bit young to label a rapist and murderer.'

'Yes, Sarge. Sorry. I'll try and be better.' I went to leave the room.

'I haven't finished yet, Blandford. Sit down.'

I did as I was told, and he took the seat behind his desk. 'Sarge, if this is about Leo . . . Doctor Stanhope . . . I didn't know he was married. I didn't know about the child . . . ' To my horror, I almost started to cry. Only the fear of seeming weak in front of the sarge stopped me. 'And it's over now, so I haven't done anything wrong.'

'No one has said you've done anything wrong, Blandford.' The sarge's voice was gentler. 'Only your mother telephoned me last night, worried out of her mind.'

I scoffed. 'Really?'

'Yes, really. I gather things are awkward there at the moment.'

'She has a boyfriend.'

'I see. Well, realising you would probably like to get away for a while until the dust settles, I've got an alternative for you. In fact it's something you should have done last year, but things got a bit hectic. How do you fancy spending a few weeks at the seaside?'

'A holiday? But Sarge, I'm not due any holidays.'

'No, not a holiday. You'd be working. I'm sending you to stay with Sergeant Enid Markham on the east coast. She runs the women's service there. You'll help with controlling the holiday crowd, plus you'll be a pretty face on the beat and the top brass are eager to show the, shall we say, more feminine side of policing.'

'Wouldn't it be better to show that we're good at our jobs, rather than just pretty faces?' I asked.

'One step at a time, Blandford. Some revolutions take years to come about. For now, you are in the police force, and you are a good-looking girl, so the top brass are looking to you to be an ambassador.'

'Do I get a say in whether I go?' I asked.

'Last night you couldn't wait to be away from Stony End. If you'd rather stay, I can always arrange it.'

'No. Sorry, Sarge. Of course I'll go. I'm not much use here the way things are. But what about the Paisley Scarf case?'

'We'll manage without you. We did get on okay, you know, for quite a few years before you turned up.' The sarge's lips curled at the corners.

I was not too happy about that, but I could not argue the logic of it. 'I'll go, Sarge. Just tell me when.'

'Tomorrow?'

I don't know why I got the impression he was trying to get rid of me, but I agreed and everything was arranged in record quick time.

At eight o'clock the following morning, I was on my way to Scarborough.

12

The sun was warm overhead and a stiff breeze blew in from the sea, helping me to feel a little less overheated in my thick dark uniform. But where the sun hit my shoulder blades, I could feel the beginnings of prickly heat. I longed to find a lamp-post on which to scratch, but I knew that was not a good way for an officer of the law to be seen. Besides, PC Steve Brown walked alongside me, and I did not want to appear weak in front of him.

Behind us were the eleventh-century ruins of Scarborough castle. South bay curved towards it, as family groups sat on the beach eating ice creams or drinking tea from jugs that could be bought from the promenade. It's odd that when I remember those times I remember them in black and white or sepia. You might be surprised to learn we did have colour in those days. It had just not seeped onto our photographs or televisions.

Hardly anyone wore bathing suits then, and bikinis were generally only seen in Hollywood movies. Women wore sundresses, often with cardigans over the top, and the men mostly wore shirts and trousers. Some would not even take their ties off, though they might roll up their trouser legs if it got a bit too warm. The working classes had not quite learned how to enjoy themselves, always afraid that someone might be watching and judging.

Children, on the other hand, ran around in their underwear or, if they were very young, in heavy terry-towelling nappies that hung down their legs. And boy did the children run, as far and as fast as they could. No one worried then that danger was around every corner. It was a more innocent time. That is not to say everyone was innocent. We just did not know that there was darkness in Britain's streets.

Along the seafront, charabancs were parked, with big signs in the windows declaring them to be part of some church group or another. Fed-up bus drivers sat smoking cigarettes, waiting for everyone to come back at five o'clock sharp. As we walked, the 109 seafront service, with its open-top deck, passed us by.

'I must take a trip on that one day,' I told Steve. I don't know why seeing everything from the top deck of a bus seemed better. It just did.

The aroma of fish and chips filled the air and my mouth watered at the tangy vinegar smell. Lunch was a while away yet. Other stalls sold fresh cockles and mussels. Nearly every shop and café was individual, with no coffee or fast food chains. There was Woolworths of course, but no British town would have been complete without it.

Appropriately, Del Shannon's 'Runaway' was playing in one of the cafés that we passed on our beat. I had been in Scarborough for a week and had known Steve for just a little under that, and I still felt as if I was running from something.

My first stop in Scarborough had been at the home of Sergeant Enid Markham, in a suburb just outside Scarborough, where I was to lodge. The house was a newly built brick building with airy rooms and a long garden, overlooking the North Yorkshire Moors. My first reaction on meeting Sergeant Markham was terror. She was a dark-haired woman who, I found, did not suffer fools gladly.

'You'll sleep in the back room,' she told me. 'I expect everyone to be in bed by ten o'clock. Breakfast is at seven o'clock every morning, without exception. You'll eat lunch out on the beat, and then supper is at seven o'clock in the evening. On the dot. I'll accept no excuses for lateness.'

'What if I'm involved in a case?' I asked. Annabel and I ate whenever we could, because we both worked long hours. I was not used to such rules.

Even my mother, who was a stickler for the niceties, understood that sometimes one had to work late.

'Then you miss supper. It's as simple as that.'

I did not understand her intransigence then, but I soon would.

I had missed supper the night before, and by just five minutes, because my bicycle had got a puncture. I also missed my Vespa, but I had not been able to bring that with me. When I arrived back at the house, Sergeant Markham and her husband, Malcolm, were already sitting down to their meal.

'Is mine in the oven?' I asked hopefully. 'I can fetch it myself. I had a puncture on the way home, and I've had to push the bike the rest of the way.'

'It's in the bin,' said Mr Markham curtly. 'It has been since just after seven.'

'It's only just after seven now.'

'I did tell you,' said Sergeant Markham. She at least had the grace to look embarrassed. She glanced from me to her husband. 'I suppose we could . . . '

'We could not,' said Mr Markham. 'She was told the times. And I warned you, Enid. If you insist on having this career of yours, then my food must still be on the table at the same time.'

'Yes, Malcolm, but . . . '

'You could always resign,' said Malcolm. He picked up his newspaper and that was it.

'You shouldn't have been late,' Sergeant Markham snapped, but I sensed sadness and humiliation behind her eyes.

I would have gone out to get fish and chips, but I'd already walked miles that day. My legs were killing me and the nearest chip shop was about a mile away. So I went up to my room and sat miserable and hungry until it was time to go to bed.

I had left Stony End for this. If I had been at home, Annabel would have made me cheese on toast, just as I did for her if she was late. But Stony End was where Leo was, with his wife and his child. I would go hungry rather than return.

'He's a tyrant,' Steve told me when I complained to him the next day as we walked the beat. Steve Brown was tall, and good-looking, with fair hair and blue eyes. He was about twenty-eight and had been a policeman for seven. He was going places. He had not told me that. Others had. Soon Steve would be off to Scotland Yard. Yet he was still approachable. I had been used to other men in the force treating me with disdain, but he had become my friend from the first day I arrived.

'You don't have to tell me,' I said. 'I'm just so surprised, because she's the tyrant at the station. But put her in a room with him, and it's like Delilah cutting all Samson's hair off. But with him as Delilah.'

'Now there's a thought,' said Steve, his eyes twinkling. 'Anyway, are you ready for your undercover operation this afternoon?'

'Yes, I suppose so. I can hardly wait,'

I said in blank tones.

A few hours later, after a hefty lunch that made up for my missed supper, I was wearing one of my best summer dresses. It was a white halter-neck with a blue forget-me-not pattern. Miniskirts had not yet been invented, though skirts were getting shorter. Those of us who lived in the sixties were still looking for our own identity, away from the Teddy Boys and Bobby Soxers, and even further away from our parents' favourites, Matt Munro and Pat Boone. But it was fair to say that I looked the epitome of a nineteen fifties female, with my hair up in a ponytail, and ankle-length socks.

I ambled through Peasholm Park. It was a beautiful park decorated in Japanese style, with a pretty pagoda and oriental bridge leading to an island in the middle of the lake. It was my job to walk around the lake, looking as if I was just enjoying the day. Plain-clothes policemen, of which Steve was one, walked ahead of and behind me.

'The minute you see him do it, blow on your whistle,' Steve had said. 'We'll be there straight away.'

I'd been given a very vague description of the man we wanted. He was thin and scrawny and wore an army great coat. Under that he wore . . . well apparently not much else, if the ladies whom he had revealed himself to were to be believed. It was my job to act as bait and help to catch him before that could happen.

I'd been walking for an hour, cursing my black court shoes and the socks whose seams were cutting into my foot, before I saw a possible. It was an elderly man in a great coat sitting on one of the benches. I had passed the bench three times, and the first two times he had not been there.

I slowed my pace and walked past him. Nothing. He just looked up at me and smiled. So I went around the lake again, still cursing my shoes and socks, and past him again. That time he spoke to me.

'I hear there's been a flasher around,' he said.

'Has there?' I was aware of Steve moving towards me with speed.

'Yes, but the police are so bloody obvious, I doubt he'll come out today.' The old man grinned, stood up and walked off, keeping his coat firmly closed around him.

'Damn,' said Steve.

We had no choice but to admit defeat and return to the station. The elderly man might well have been our perpetrator, but my cover was blown, as was Steve's and our colleagues'.

'Who'd have thought a flasher would have half a brain?' I said after we had changed back into our uniforms and drank tea in the canteen. 'I felt a bit sorry for him though.'

'Come on, Bobbie,' said Steve. 'You must know that flashers will often move on to more serious sex crimes.'

'Yes, I know. I've read all the research. It's just that he seemed more as if he needed friendship. I'm not saying he's going the right way about it, but he's probably on his own all day. No one will talk to him because he's old and a bit smelly-looking. So he might do the only thing he can to get their attention.'

'I'll remember that if you ever start ignoring me,' Steve said with a wicked grin.

'You're young enough for me to knee in the groin,' I warned him. 'And believe me, I have a very sharp knee.'

'Yeah, you know I never would, don't you, Bobbie?'

'I should hope not.'

'So . . . ' He paused a moment and I wondered what was coming next. 'So now I've had due warning, how about coming out for a drink with me tonight after work?'

'I daren't. If I'm late for supper again . . . '

'I'll buy you chips at the corner café on North Bay.'

'Ooh, the last of the big spenders.'

'I'll throw in a meat pie.'

'I don't know,' I said more seriously. 'The thing is, Steve, I've only just got out of a relationship. That's why I'm here. I'm running away.'

'What happened?'

'His wife.'

'Ah. Well, I don't have a wife, and he doesn't deserve you.'

'It's not like that.' I was as surprised as Steve to find myself defending Leo. 'I mean, he thought the marriage had ended, but she turned up again. With a child. I can't compete with that. I'm not ready to date again.'

'Very well. Something less threatening than a date. It's our day off tomorrow. How about I take you and show you where Anne Brontë is buried?'

'You really know how to show a girl a good time!' I laughed. 'Pie and chips and Anne Brontë's grave!'

'No, seriously. Girls like that stuff. Or so I'm told.'

'So you're told?'

'Yeah, I asked some of the blokes how I could impress you. One of them said Anne Brontë's grave.'

'I take it he's a bachelor.'

'Now you come to mention it . . . '

'Anyway, why would you want to impress me, Steve?'

'I'd have thought that was obvious. You're gorgeous, funny and clever.'

'Thank you. It's very sweet of you to say so.'

'Don't say that.'

'Why? You are sweet.'

'Because it's usually followed by, 'You're just like a brother to me, Steve.' Have you no sympathy, woman? You might as well just stab me in the eye and have done with.'

I could not help laughing. I tried to remember if Leo and I had ever laughed so much together, but our relationship had been fraught with difficulties from the very beginning.

'We'll go and see Anne Brontë's grave,' I said, coming to a decision. 'I'll make a picnic for us.'

'Brilliant! Now I've got to dash. I've got my report to fill in.' Steve reached over and kissed me on the cheek.

I felt a flutter of something, but I had been in love with Leo for so long, I did not know exactly how Steve made me feel.

13

The Church of St. Mary in Scarborough was built in the twelfth century on the castle headland. It had been built and rebuilt many times over the years. The churchyard was pretty, with many old headstones. Steve and I spent ages looking at them all, including Anne Brontë's.

She had travelled from Haworth to Scarborough in eighteen forty-eight, hoping the sea air would help her consumption. Three days after arriving she died, aged just twenty-nine. Her tombstone mistakenly said she was twenty-eight, but this would not be corrected until nineteen ninety-nine. Not that the extra year made much difference.

'Either way, it's so young,' I said to Steve. The day was dull, but warm. 'All of the Brontës died young, except the father. Yet when you read their books, you feel as though they lived several life times. They had so much wisdom for women who had hardly lived at all.'

'Can't say I've ever read them,' said Steve.

'Not even at school?'

'Nah, I like science fiction best. Isaac Asimov. Ray Bradbury.'

'Oh yes, me too,' I said, eagerly. 'But the classics are classic for a reason. They're proper stories, with clear ideas of good and bad. This world seems to be losing that certainty. Sorry, I'm preaching a bit, aren't I?'

'Preach all you want. I could listen to your voice all day, Bobbie.'

I moved away from Anne Brontë's headstone and along the path towards others. Most of the stones were for people who had been dead over a hundred years. The sea air had worked away at the tombstones, leaving them uneven. Still, I thought as I looked out over the headland, I could not think of a more beautiful place to be buried. If the world stopped now, I thought, I would not be too sorry. I would not have to go back to the awful Markhams' house. I would not have to deal with my feelings for Leo and Steve.

I had moved on to another path, as much to put distance between myself and Steve as anything else. His presence unnerved me.

We always believe that if we are desperately in love with someone, then we cannot be attracted to anyone else. This is not true. As they say in Derbyshire, just because you're on a diet it doesn't mean you can't look at cream cakes. Steve was handsome, charming, and he made me laugh. What's more, everything seemed so uncomplicated with him.

'Hey, wait a minute,' he said, catching up with me. 'You move quickly for a woman with such short legs.'

'I just want to see as much as possible,' I lied. I stopped in front of one of the gravestones, having no choice but to wait for him. That was when I noticed that the headstone was slightly newer. But that was not really what caught my notice. It was the name — *Harold York died 16 December 1914*. He had been just sixteen years old. Several other graves alongside had the same date.

'That must have been when the Germans raided Scarborough,' said Steve. 'Nineteen people died. Lots more were lost along the coast towards Hartlepool and Whitby.'

'It's the name,' I said. 'Not the circumstances. We've been looking for a man called Harold York in Stony End. One woman was connected to him before she died. Another woman was seeing a man called George Clarence. It's a name that Harold York used for conning people.' I explained the whole story to Steve, including the most recent murder. 'Not only that, but the unknown woman wore clothes that might have come from a Scarborough shop. I wonder if this Harold York is related to our Harold York.'

'We had a murder like that in Scarborough before the war,' Steve told me. 'I was only a kid at the time, but it happened to one of my grandmother's neighbours. I remember her saying that a girl on her street was strangled. I don't know if a Paisley scarf was involved.'

'Would your grandmother remember about it now?'

'Oh yes. In fact, she does most of her remembering about the past. It's the present she's not too good at.'

I was reminded of Mrs Atkins, back at the care home, who was much the same way. I had left without telling her what happened to her bike. Perhaps that was just as well. She might prefer not to know that it had possibly been used to escape a murder scene.

We ate our picnic of Spam sandwiches and boiled eggs, washed down with Robertson's Orange Squash, sitting in the castle grounds. The sea was choppy, and I could have sat and watched it all day.

'Let's go and see my grandmother,' Steve suggested. 'She'll have a cake baked for tea and we can ask her if she knew Harold York.'

'It's so good of you to take an interest, Steve.' Cake was one thing I had missed since leaving Stony End. If Annabel and I didn't have a slab of cake at the cottage, we could always rely on Greta and Mrs Higgins to make us some. Sergeant Markham was not much for baking cakes. I doubted she had time. The cake she did buy was from the shop and not nearly as nice as homemade.

'I wouldn't be a policeman if crime didn't interest me. Come on.'

It turned out that Steve's grandmother, Netta Brown, was rather more alert than he had claimed. She owned a guest house on West Square, directly opposite the Scarborough train station. The houses were in a horseshoe formation set around a neat little garden, in which holiday-makers rested with their luggage either on their way to or from the train station.

Netta's house was a four-storey whitewashed building in the centre of the square. A sign in the window declared there were vacancies.

From Steve's description of her, I had expected a frail old woman, but Netta turned out to be a sprightly lady. 'Steve's mum was sixteen when she had him,' Netta explained as we sat around the tea table in her private sitting room. She had shouted a series of commands to her staff before leading us through. I imagined she would be terrifying as an employer. 'Married, of course.' At the time I did not notice how odd it was that she said that. 'Daphne was far too young, and too small in the pelvis. She didn't stand a chance. She died a few days later and his dad, who was in the Merchant Navy, had to go back to work. He died during the war. Steve never even knew him, did you, duck? So I've raised my grandson. Even gave him my surname.'

'You did a good job,' I said, accepting a slice of Battenberg cake and a cup of strong, sweet tea.

Netta preened a little and touched

her hair. 'Yes, I did, if I may so say myself. Now, what did you want to ask me about? Steve said it was about Violet Johnson.'

'Was that her name?' I quickly explained to Netta about the murders in Stony End, and Harold York. 'Did you ever know a man of that name?'

'I went to school with a boy who had that name,' said Netta. 'But he died when the Germans bombed the east coast.'

'Yes, we saw his grave up at the churchyard,' I said. 'Did he have family? A cousin or a younger brother with the same name, perhaps?'

'Not that I know of.'

'What can you tell me about Violet Johnson?'

'Hmm, well, young Violet was no better than she should have been. Her mother owned a B and B on the other side of the square, but well, Mrs Johnson was not always very strict about her clientele. As long as she was making money she didn't care if they were married or not, and there were some rumours that she rented rooms out by the hour, if you get my drift.' Netta sniffed to show her disapproval. 'It's no wonder the girl ran wild. She — Violet, that is — started running around with the young airmen who were stationed in the area. They used to train up near Flamborough Head. And it was fair to say that all the young girls liked hanging around them. Then one night, just before the war started properly, Violet was found strangled.'

'Do you know who she might have been seeing at the time?'

'Well, there were several men. That was the point. Some girls ask for it.'

'It was hardly her fault she was murdered,' I said quietly. 'Even if she was a little . . . loose . . . it doesn't mean that she deserved to die.'

'She had a child, you know. Born out of wedlock, of course. A girl, Harriet. She's another wild one. She went off months ago, possibly with some bloke. Bad blood will out. I can't say she's missed around here.'

'I know it's unlikely, but would you happen to have a picture of Violet Johnson? Or perhaps her mother might. Which B and B was it?'

'Oh, the Johnsons left that place years ago. Mrs Johnson lives in a flat on the seafront now. Living off her immoral earnings, if you ask me.'

Netta's self-righteousness was getting on my nerves a little. 'Do you have a picture?'

'Yes, I do. My girl, Daphne, used to be at school with Violet. They were good friends, but had a falling out. I can't say I'm sorry. I've got an old class photo somewhere. You wait here and I'll find it.'

Steve had said nothing whilst his grandmother was in the room. Only when she left us did he say, 'It's all rubbish, of course.'

'What? About Violet Johnson?'

'No, about my mother. It's true I never knew my father, but he and my mother were never married. Grandma just likes people to think she was.'

'Oh. I'm sorry.'

'I'm just explaining, because I know she's a bit of a hypocrite. She builds Mum up as a real paragon of virtue. When really she wasn't.'

'Why? Because she trusted that a man would do the right thing by her if she gave in to him? Women are allowed to make mistakes, Steve, just as much as men are.'

'And what mistakes have you made? Go on, tell me.' He looked at me with interest.

'I'm not talking about me.' I dropped my eyes, and spent several seconds concentrating on the blue rose pattern on Netta's Pyrex tea service. It was smooth and shiny but there was a tiny sliver missing from one of the side plates, which I knew from experience could turn out to be dangerously sharp.

Steve and his grandmother's attitude felt much the same way. Though friendly, there was a sharpness to them that worried me. What might they think of the mistakes I had made in life? If I turned up dead one day, would they say that I had it coming?

I thought of Leo and how accepting he had been about the Italian. But with Steve I would have to tell him about the Italian and Leo. My indiscretions were piling up, and whilst I had come to terms with the mistakes I had made, the way Steve and his grandmother talked caused the shame to rise up in me. To them I was damaged goods, and I hated being in that position.

'Sorry,' said Steve, putting his hand over mine. His touch burned me, and not in the hot passionate way that Leo's had. 'I didn't mean to pry. You've obviously had your heart broken and it's clear you're a decent lass.'

'Oh well, I shouldn't turn up murdered then, should I?' I said bitterly.

'What's that supposed to mean?'

'It means that as a policeman, you should be on the victim's side, regardless of the mistakes they've made in their lives. It makes me so angry that

188

men can behave any way they want, and it's doubtful their sex life would be taken into account if they were murdered. But if a woman who's been around the block a bit is murdered, people think she deserves it. She's failed to live up to the saintly ideal of womanhood. But she doesn't deserve it. Don't you see? No one deserves to have their lives taken away from them like that. Not because of who they sleep with.'

'You're really gorgeous when you're angry.'

'I'm going outside for some fresh air.' If I had stayed in that room, I might have slapped him. The sitting room had French doors leading onto a terrace, so I went through those and down into the garden. The air had become muggy and I sensed a storm was on the way, but it was nothing compared to the storm inside me.

I felt so angry on behalf of the women who had died. They had all been looking for something, whether it was love, stability or simply the means of eating a square meal the next day. And they had been punished for it, because they had not behaved in the way that people thought women should. Some man had come along and taken advantage of their vulnerability. I wanted more than ever to catch him and make him pay for his sins, which were far greater than those the women had committed.

'Bobbie, I have the photographs,' Netta called from the French doors.

I turned and put on my brightest smile. I was a guest in her house and so far I had not behaved well in the way I had judged her. I silently vowed to improve that.

I had to sit through a lot of photographs that meant nothing to me, but Netta seemed happy to relish the memories so I let her talk. 'That was my great-great uncle Brian. We don't talk about him,' she said of one picture. She did not elaborate on why they did not talk about him. 'He went to South America and good riddance, I say

. . . That was Aunt Penelope. She ran a tea shop in the town. Her seed cake was renowned all over Yorkshire. These are my cousins, Pamela, Doreen and Adeline, with their little brother, Henry. They'd come over from South America on a visit. Was it just after or just before the Great War? I don't remember now.'

'So they were Great-uncle Brian's family?'

'Yes, granddaughters. But we didn't hold it against them. They were second or third cousins. Might even have been fourth. I'm not sure how it all works.'

There was something familiar about young Henry. I looked from him to Steve then back again. 'You look alike,' I said.

Netta looked up, alarmed. 'Oh no. No, I don't think so.' I did not know why she was so disturbed. It was natural for relatives to resemble each other.

'Did erm . . . Did Henry ever visit again?' I asked. 'When he was older?'

'No.' The word shot from Netta's lips like a bullet from a gun.

'But my mother visited South America in the thirties though, didn't she, Grandma?' Steve asked. 'I remember you telling me.'

'She went for a summer, yes. The girls had taken a shine to her when they visited, so they paid for her to go over as soon as she was old enough to travel alone.'

I may or may not have stumbled upon the truth about Steve's father, because he and young Henry did look very much alike. But that was not where I had recognised Henry from. The familiarity was linked to something or someone else. I could not remember who or where.

'Are you related to the Markhams at all?' I asked, trying to bring up Malcolm Markham's face in my mind. I had been staying at the house for over a week, yet his jowly features were still hard to recall. All I could conjure up was a bullish neck and a sweaty brow.

'Not as far as we know,' Netta replied.

'That can't be it then. I just feel as if I've seen Henry somewhere else, that's all.'

'He must have one of those faces.'

'I suppose so.'

'And here it is. The picture of Daphne and Violet at school.'

Like all class photographs, it was hard to tell one face from another, yet Netta pointed confidently to her daughter, Daphne, and Violet Johnson. They were in the second row, near to the middle. Daphne had been tall and fair, like her son and her mother. Violet, on the other hand, had been shorter. It was hard to make out her hair colour on the black and white photo. 'What colour was Violet's hair?' I asked.

'Auburn,' said Netta. 'A bit darker than yours. Brassy-looking, if you ask me.'

'What, mine?' I asked, mischievously.

'No, no, of course not. You're a nice girl, Bobbie. Anyone can see that.'

I smiled at her. If only she knew. 'I wonder if there are any newer pictures of her at the station,' I said to Steve. 'There must be something in the file.'

'We could look tomorrow.'

'If you're not fed up with all this,' I said.

'No, not at all. That poor girl's murderer should be caught.'

I did not ask him about his change of heart. I just decided that he was inconsistent and I could not trust him.

14

Violet Johnson's mother, Mabel, lived in a flat above a chip shop. It was on a side street just off the seafront, and the sea could just about be viewed from one side of the bow window, in between an amusement arcade and a pub. Unable to get Violet out of my mind, I had gone there alone to speak to Mrs Johnson and ask for her version of events.

The flat smelled of stale beer, stale cabbage and yesterday's fish and chips. Mrs Johnson sat huddled in front of a one-bar electric fire despite the warm day, wearing several layers of clothes. Like many alcoholics whose digestive systems had been ruined, she had a habit of hiccupping or belching every couple of words. 'They all looked down on us . . . on that street. Especially . . . Netta Brown. She always was stuck-up. As if anyone believes . . . that her daughter was married to . . . a merchant seaman. Netta used the same excuse when she gave birth to Daphne, and none of us were fooled then. I can't stand . . . these people who put on airs and graces, as if they're better than everyone else. She's had her fair share of unmarried couples staying overnight, I can tell you. She just pretends not to know. Can I get you a beer or a stout?'

'No thank you, Mrs Johnson. I'm on duty later and if Sergeant Markham smells alcohol on my breath, she'll have my guts for garters.' It was not strictly true, but everything in Mrs Johnson's flat was so grimy, I did not want to drink out of anything, not even shop-bought bottles of ale.

'Do you mind if I . . . ?'

'No, not at all.' I doubted that Mrs Johnson would have agreed if I had asked her not to drink.

She snapped the lid off a bottle and drank straight from it. Such a sight was shocking, even to me. Most women drank out of a glass, and a special ladies' glass at that. 'I never used to . . . drink. I ran a tight ship, and maybe sometimes I did let people use the hotel rooms for an hour or so, but they were tough times, the thirties. I couldn't afford to turn down clientele and everyone else was looking for a few moments of happiness. But my place was always clean.'

I looked around the flat dubiously.

'Oh I know what you're thinking, but I wasn't like this either. An old soak, scraping an existence on what I have left from selling the business. Then my girl died and . . . you don't know what it's like, WPC Blandford, to lose a child. You seem a nice girl, so I pray you never do. You're supposed to go before them, leaving a few grandchildren to carry on the family name. He took that from me, the killer. He took my girl and any hopes I had of the future, so if I do sit here sometimes and drink a bit too much, it's only because I have nothing to hope for now. I'm just counting the days till I can be with my girl again.'

I swallowed back a lump in my throat. 'I'm so sorry,' I said. 'Do you know who your daughter was seeing at the time?'

'She had a few beaux, but I didn't know them all. Just before the war, people just came and went as they moved around the country, taking up their places. I don't say my Violet was an angel, but she was choosy about who she went out with. She liked a man with a posh accent. There was that one, an RAF man. He had the gift of the gab.'

'Harold York?' I asked.

'No, no, Harold York was a young boy who died when the Germans shelled the beach. In the Great War. He wouldn't have been alive then. It was another name. Oh . . . It's like York but not.'

'Leeds?' I asked, frowning.

'No, don't be silly.' For the first time, Mrs Johnson laughed. 'What was it? Gloucester. That's it. Richard Glouces-ter. Dickie.'

I groaned inwardly. Was this another pseudonym of Harold York or a different man entirely? Harold York, George Clarence, Richard Gloucester . . . The names meant something as a whole, but I could not quite work out why. Chances were that they all came off a gravestone somewhere, and the real man, whoever he was, had a completely different name. This would make him very difficult to track down.

'I realise this is difficult, but can you tell me anything about the night your daughter died, Mrs Johnson?'

'It was in August, just before the war broke out properly. We already had our gas masks, and some places had curfews at night. Violet was talking about joining the land army. I didn't know what I was going to do, but we knew that it would be difficult to entice people to the seaside, particularly one on the east coast. This man, Richard Gloucester, showed up on the back doorstep. Oh, he was handsome. I remember joking that if I was a few years younger . . . ' She smiled sadly at the memory. 'I wish it had been me now. They went out, and Violet disappeared for a few days. Well, that had happened before, so I thought nothing of it to begin with. Then I had a feeling that something was wrong. She usually telephoned or turned up. They found her up the coast.' Mrs Johnson lapsed into silence for a while. 'She had been strangled, with a Paisley scarf.'

'Was it hers?'

'What?'

'The scarf. Was it hers?'

'Yes, of course it was hers. She didn't steal it.'

'I'm sorry,' I said. 'I didn't mean to suggest she had. Only the other ladies who died didn't own the scarves they were strangled with.'

'Oh, I see. Well, yes, I'm sure it was hers. At least she was wearing it when she went out.'

'Mrs Johnson?'

'Yes?'

'You said that when your daughter died it left you with nothing, not even grandchildren. But you have a granddaughter, don't you?'

'Humph, you mean Harriet? That stuck-up little madam wanted nothing to do with me when she grew up. She went to work at that department store in the town, working as a mannequin.'

'A mannequin?'

'Yes, walking up and down to show women how clothes look. She's got the legs for it, and a good figure. Anyway, I haven't seen her for years.'

'How old would she be now?'

'Twenty-nine. Or thirty. I forget. Why?'

'Do you have a picture of her?'

'I might.' Reluctantly, Mrs Johnson got up from her chair and shuffled over to the large oak sideboard. 'I thought we'd be together, with only having each other, but she didn't want to know me. Once she told me that if not for me, Violet wouldn't be dead. Can you believe that?'

'People say terrible things when they're heart-broken,' I said in consoling tones. 'Losing her mother must have hurt her dreadfully.'

'I don't think she even cared. All she wanted to know, when she was old enough, was if her mother had left her anything. There she is, in the newspaper. I cut that out last Christmas. I don't know why. It's not like I'm bothered . . . '

I took the cutting from Mrs Johnson. It was from a local paper and advertised a fashion show at the department store. And standing there, dressed in what appeared to be a grey suit like the one Kim Novak wore in Vertigo, was Harriet Johnson.

She was also the woman we had found dead on the Stony End castle grounds.

15

I did not want to say anything to Mrs Johnson until I was certain that Harriet Johnson was the dead woman. The poor woman had already lost her daughter in terrible circumstances. I did not want to be the one to tell her that her granddaughter had also been murdered, and possibly by the same man. Because I was sure now that it was the same man. The coincidence was too much.

I called into the department store on my way home and asked to speak to the manager, Mrs Scattergood. 'Yes, I can confirm that Harriet Johnson worked here up until recently,' she said. She was a capable-looking woman in her late thirties. We sat in her walnut-lined office. She barked an order at an adenoidal teenage girl, called Esme, to bring coffee. The coffee was quick coming, but tasted bitter. 'I'm still training Esme in the art of coffee-making,' said Mrs Scattergood, grimacing. She smiled at me, one professional woman to another, and I felt as if I was part of a secret society.

'You said recently?' I asked. 'About Harriet Johnson.'

'It's a pity she left. She was one of our better models. Not classically beautiful, but she had good legs, and the sort of face one forgot easily. Oh that sounds rather bitchy, doesn't it? But the point with shop mannequins is that you don't want them to have too much personality of their own. The clothes they wear have to speak for themselves. But a couple of months ago, Harriet handed in her notice. She said that she had found better prospects elsewhere.'

'Did she say where?'

'No. In fact, she didn't even ask me for a reference, which seemed strange. She was a peculiar girl.'

'In what way?'

'Her mother was murdered just before the war, you know.'

'Yes, I did know.'

'Ah, well, Harriet was always very cold about it. I don't know if she was hiding the heartache, or if she really didn't care. It was like there was something missing with her. Some of the girls cry at the drop of a hat — literally, in the clothing department — and of course one doesn't want that sort of thing too much. But Harriet could be as cold as ice, when other girls got married or had babies. She didn't mix well, and had very few friends outside work. She didn't socialise with the others at all. I gather she was estranged from her grandmother.'

'Yes, sadly.' It seemed to me that Harriet Johnson was estranged from everybody. I had wondered how a woman could just go missing and no one notice. Now I knew.

'What has happened, WPC Blandford?'

'I'm afraid I can't confirm anything yet. But I wonder . . . to save Mrs Johnson any more anguish . . . if I need you to identify a body.'

Mrs Scattergood put her hands to her mouth. 'Oh my goodness. I had no idea it was anything like that. I mean . . . well, I suppose I can say it now . . . sometimes things went missing from the stock — small things like stockings and scarves — and for a while I did suspect Harriet. I had no proof, and then she resigned . . . ' She spread her hands out as if to illustrate the breadth of the problem. 'I thought she had been caught stealing in her new job, is what I'm trying to say.'

'No, it's nothing like that.' I explained briefly to Mrs Scattergood about the woman in the castle grounds and how I now believed it was Harriet Johnson. She understood the situation immediately and I knew I could trust her to be discreet.

I had time to make a quick telephone call to Sergeant Simmonds in Stony End, before heading back to the Markhams' house.

'That's a turn-up for the books,' said the sarge, his voice crackling down the long-distance line. 'I'll look into it and see if we can't get a positive identification.'

'When will you know?' I asked.

'Not yet, Blandford. We're not sitting on our haunches here waiting for you to return, you know. We've had an old man attacked and a break-in at the boarding house this weekend.'

'What old man?'

'Mr Rodgers, from the estate.'

'Really? What happened?'

I sensed that the sarge was hesitating before he spoke. 'Nothing to concern you, Blandford.' He put the phone down without saying goodbye, leaving me wondering what on earth had happened to Mr Rodgers.

As I entered the kitchen, at dead on seven o'clock, I saw Mr Markham standing over the waste bin with a steaming plate of liver and onions in his hands. I snatched it from him and said, 'Seems like I'm just in the nick of time,' before going straight to the dining room.

Sergeant Markham, who had presumably heard me, sat open-mouthed. Mr Markham followed me in and slumped down in his own chair. If looks could kill, I would not be able to tell this story, but thankfully they cannot and I was not going to be intimidated by him.

'There have been some amazing developments,' I said to Sergeant Markham, and began to tell her what I had found out.

'We don't talk policing at this table,' said Mr Markham. 'Not in this house.'

'I was under the impression that this was a police house,' I said cheerfully, 'and that it came with the job. So I can't think of anywhere better.'

That did earn me a murderous look, but I'd had enough of men like Mr Markham. It was men like him who upheld attitudes about womanhood that led to the deaths of the women in my case. He may not be a murderer himself, but the poison was within him and that spread to other men, who had less control over their actions.

'Hush,' said Sergeant Markham, her cheeks reddening. 'Just eat your food in silence please, Blandford.'

As she was my superior, I had no choice but to do as I was told. Not really feeling hungry, but determined not to let Mr Markham win this one, I swallowed down the liver and onions, each bite landing heavy on my stomach.

After I had helped Sergeant Markham wash the dishes, I went upstairs to my room, out of the way. Five minutes later she followed me and entered without knocking. I sat on the chair in front of the dressing table, looking at the picture of my dad that I took everywhere with me. I half-turned and waited for the telling-off I knew was coming.

Instead she sat on the end of the bed. 'It's been hard for Malcolm since he came out of work,' she said. 'No man wants to think that his wife keeps him, so he likes to rule the roost at home. And I allow him that because . . . '

'It makes life easier.'

'In a nutshell, yes.'

'But you work hard. I work hard. We also can't always guarantee what hours we're going to be working. It isn't for me to tell you how to run your home, Sergeant Markham, but I gather you're being paid extra to have me here. So I do have a right to eat when I return from work. I don't mind warmed-up dinners. I don't even mind cooking my own food if it's very late. I certainly don't expect you to wait up for me. But I don't think it's right that my food — which has been paid for by the police force — should go in the bin because I'm just a few minutes late.'

'I'll talk to Malcolm about it, but he does expect the rules of his house to be followed.'

'It's not his house,' I murmured. 'It's yours.'

'As I said, it's been difficult for him. I don't want to emasculate him any more than he has been already.' She spread out her hands and for the first time showed a hint of vulnerability. 'Please help me. You'll be leaving here at the end of the season, but I have to stay. I have to live with him.'

I saw fear in Sergeant Markham's eyes and I began to wonder what happened in the house when there were no lodgers to bear witness.

'I'm sorry,' I said, feeling awful. 'I had no idea.' I wanted to suggest that she leave him and go somewhere safe, but it was not the done thing to interfere in a marriage then. There were few places an abused woman could go, and even the police would not get involved in instances of domestic abuse. An Englishman's home truly was his castle, and he could treat the people in it in any way he chose. 'I'll do my best to stick to the rules,' I promised, even though every instinct in my body railed against it. I hated the idea of a man like Malcolm Markham ruling me, but I also saw it as my duty to protect Sergeant Markham in any way I could.

'I'd like to know about the case,' said Sergeant Markham. 'I remember when

Violet Johnson died, just before the war. I was fairly new to the service then, so had no say in anything, but the case was thrown aside when the war started.'

'The same with Ruth Yates and Betty Norris,' I said, nodding. 'Added to which they had bad reputations, so no one cared. And now it seems that Violet's daughter, Harriet, has been murdered by the same man.' I shook my head, not really sure what I was saying no to. Perhaps it was to the atrocious treatment of women, and to the double standards of men.

'Well, do keep me informed of any developments. Just . . . '

'Not in this house.'

'Yes. Thank you for understanding, Bobbie.'

It was the first time she had used my name. 'I'm not sure I do understand,' I said.

'That's because you're a modern young woman. But you wait till you fall in love and want to give your all to a man.'

'I've already been in love,' I said, not admitting I still was in love with Leo. 'But I wasn't aware of having to give up myself for him.'

Sergeant Markham left me as there was not much else for us to say. I wished I were back in Stony End. Though I had only lived there for a year, I was homesick for all the old familiar faces. Homesick for Annabel, who would always want to hear my news. Homesick for the friends I had made at the station. Homesick for Greta and Mrs Higgins. Homesick for Leo . . .

I pushed the thought away. There was no point in thinking of him. He had a wife and child.

At around ten o'clock I started to undress, ready for bed, when Sergeant Markham knocked on my bedroom door. 'There's someone at the door for you, Blandford.' She sounded disapproving and I realised our earlier camaraderie had gone. When I opened the door, she had a warning look in her eyes. 'Malcolm is in bed,' she whispered. 'Please don't let him hear you. It's PC Brown.'

Steve? I wondered what he wanted that time of night. I went downstairs, making sure I was presentable first, and found him sitting on the garden wall.

'Things went a bit wrong the other day,' he said. 'You've been avoiding me.'

'No, I haven't. I've been busy working,' I explained. I was lying. I had been avoiding him.

'I know my grandma comes across as a bit sanctimonious — but she means well.'

I wanted to say, 'Oh that's all right then.' Lots of people had done terrible things in the spirit of meaning well. It made them look down on their neighbours and patronise others. To some people, meaning well excused a lot of bad behaviour. 'I'm sure she does,' I said instead.

'I do too. I mean that I don't really think all that stuff about women, Bobbie. It's just that when I'm with her, it rubs off, you know.'

'Then try to have your own thoughts

and feelings,' I said.

'I do. But she brought me up, you know, and it would be disrespectful to contradict her.'

'Yes, I suppose it would.'

'I have my own thoughts and feelings about you,' he said, standing up and walking over to where I stood on the pavement. I looked hastily at the house, hoping that Mr Markham was not watching. It was like having a father, but one who only ever disapproved. It occurred to me that Mr Markham and Netta Brown would make a good couple. Perhaps if I could get them together, Sergeant Markham would be happy.

'I really like you, Bobbie.'

'I like you too, Steve,' I said, but only because it was expected of me.

He stroked my cheek and I waited for that thrill that I felt whenever Leo touched me. There was nothing there. Steve might be a nice bloke, or at least a nice bloke in progress, but he was not for me.

'I know there's someone else you

care for,' he was saying.

'Don't, Steve. Don't talk about him. I can't bear it.' I wanted to cry, but stopped myself. I did not want to appear weak in front of Steve. For some reason it seemed important that he thought me strong.

'Then forget him and stick with me, Bobbie.' Steve lowered his head and it was with growing horror that I realised he was about to kiss me. I did not want him to, yet I stood rooted to the spot, feeling it would be rude to move away.

When his lips found mine, they were cold and dry, yet I could not move away. When I finally did, it was because I heard someone coughing behind me.

'Hello, Bobbie,' said an oh-so-familiar voice. Then I felt the thrill. But I also felt sick and dizzy.

I spun around. 'Leo?' He stood there in the dark, looking every bit as dark and broodingly handsome as I remembered. Poor Steve was outclassed in every way. He never stood a chance really. But Leo must have thought that because I accepted the kiss, that I was as interested in Steve as he was in me.

'I'm sorry to interrupt.' He did not look sorry. He looked furious. As if he had a right to! He was a married man with a child. 'Joe has gone missing and I was hoping he had come to you.'

16

Because even I could see how embarrassing it was that two men had turned up at my door on the same night, I took Leo to a late-night café on the seafront. Young men and women stood around the jukebox, playing an Elvis song — 'His Latest Flame' — which seemed very apt under the circumstances.

'Why did he run away?' I asked as we drank coffee. Nowadays it would probably be called something like a skinny mocha chocca latte espresso. Back then you had the choice of flat coffee or frothy coffee. We chose the latter. It came in smoked-glass cups with matching saucers.

'Norman Rodgers was attacked. He's in hospital.'

'What? When?' I was horrified, realising that was the old man that Sergeant Simmonds had been talking about. 'Surely they don't think that Joe did it?'

'They'd gone to the pub together on Saturday night. They were seen arriving together and leaving together.'

'Mr Rodgers went out? I thought he was agoraphobic.'

'Joe had been working on the garden for Rodgers, and Rodgers promised to buy Joe a half-pint of cider.' Then, as now, it was legal for a sixteen-year-old to go into a pub and drink cider as long as it was bought for them by someone over eighteen. It's a law that's always puzzled me as there is some real gut-rot cider out there, yet it is considered safer than beer or spirits. 'It was a big moment for both of them by all accounts. Everyone in the pub said they had a great time, though Mr Rodgers was a little bit quiet. Joe says that they said goodnight at around nine o'clock and he came home. But I didn't hear him come in till nearly eleven, so there's an hour unaccounted for. Anyway, the next morning the police knocked on the door, saying that Mr Rodgers had been attacked and was in hospital with a serious head injury.'

'You don't think Joe did it?' I asked again. 'Come on, Leo, he's a troubled kid but he's not violent.'

'Who knows what goes on in his head? These last few months have been difficult. Cindy-Lou tries so hard with him, but he doesn't want to know.'

'Doesn't he get on with Mikey either?' I asked, trying to stem the tide of pain that washed over me.

'Mikey isn't over here yet. He's been unwell so his grandparents didn't want him to travel.'

'I hope he's better soon. You must be dying to meet him.'

'Yes, yes I am.' There was something bleak about Leo's voice. I wanted to ask more, but I knew it would only cause me more pain. 'But for now Joe is a problem I need to solve. He likes you, Bobbie. Are you sure he hasn't been here?'

'Do you think I wouldn't have told you?'

'No, no of course not. Sorry. I've just run out of ideas.'

'What about his mother's family in Sheffield?'

'They barely have anything to do with him.'

'But you could go and ask.'

'Yes, I suppose I could. The thing is . . . ' Leo looked down at his coffee. He had not drunk any of it and it was starting to congeal in the cup. 'I wanted to see you, Bobbie, so I suppose I used Joe running away as an excuse to come here.'

'Don't, Leo. The last time I saw you, you had a wife, and unless that's changed, I can't be with you. You know that.'

'I know. I wouldn't ask you.' He grimaced. 'Damn it, Bobbie my life is not the same without you. I miss you so much.'

'I miss you too.'

'Really? Because you seemed to be having a good time without me.'

'How dare you?' I hissed. 'How dare you judge me? You have a wife, Leo. Remember? Oh, no, perhaps you don't, because you managed to forget her before.' I started to stand up, but he caught my hand.

'I'm sorry. I know I have no right to be jealous, but I am, okay? Come with me to Sheffield at least, to help me to find Joe. I know you care about him as much as I do.'

'Damn you,' I whispered. 'Damn you for manipulating me like this, Leo.' I ran out of the café, tears streaming from my eyes. He came after me and caught hold of my shoulders, spinning me around.

'I've never stopped loving you,' he said. He kissed me and for a moment I forgot Steve, I forgot Cindy-Lou, and I forgot I was supposed to be a good girl. This was what a kiss should be, I thought. Hot and passionate, and full of desire. Maybe the fact it was forbidden added to my excitement. Stolen fruit and all that. I remembered our night in London and how wonderful that had been. I wished . . . I wished . . .

I pulled away. 'We can't,' I said. 'Don't you see? It would cheapen everything we've ever felt for each other if we allowed desire to get the better of us.'

'I know.' Leo let me go and put his hands in his pockets. 'I'm just not ready for you not to be a part of my life, Bobbie.'

'I'll help you find Joe, but then you'll have to get used to it. We both will.'

It did not occur to me to explain to Sergeant and Mr. Markham where I was going. I was a grown woman after all.

It was the early hours of the morning when we reached Sheffield, after a strained trip in which every attempt at polite conversation turned into stomach-churning emotion. The last time I had been to Sheffield with Leo was when we thought Joe was in danger from a murderer. The post-war landscape was gradually being replaced by high-rise buildings such as the Park Hill flats, which had been started in nineteen fifty-seven, but some parts of the city were still flattened. Joe's family lived in one of the few houses that remained in the middle of wasteland. It was in darkness.

'We should have telephoned ahead,' I

said when we pulled up outside. 'It looks like they're all in bed.'

'Well, we're here now,' said Leo. We got out of the car and Leo went up to the front door and knocked. There was only one street light and it could barely be bothered to shine.

It took a while before anyone answered. A light in the passageway came on and the door opened. I had never met Joe's uncle and aunt because Sergeant Simmonds had sent the family to a safe house the last time we visited. A haystack of a man opened the door, wearing just pyjama trousers and a dirty white vest. Thick dark hair matted his chest, arms and hands. A rim of dark around his eyes suggested that he worked down the pit. I'd often seen the men come home with similarly 'kohled' eyes. I presumed this was Joe's uncle.

'What do you want?' he said.

'I'm Leo Stanhope. Doctor Leo Stanhope. Joe's guardian. This is WPC Bobbie Blandford. We've met before, when I came to talk to you about Joe's care. We wondered if you'd seen Joe.'

'Seen him, sent him packing.'

'What?' I heard the hiss of anger that fell from Leo's lips.

'Well he's not our problem now, is he?'

'I'm WPC Blandford of the Stony End police,' I half-lied before Leo could speak. I put my hand on his arm, afraid he might hit Joe's uncle. 'We're concerned that a sixteen-year-old boy has gone missing. Could you not have contacted Leo — Doctor Stanhope — and let him know?'

'You said you'd take all of it off our shoulders,' said the man, looking at Leo and ignoring me. 'You said we'd have no more bother. Well, what was he doing turning up here, then?'

'What time did you last see him?' I asked.

The man sniffed. 'About eight o'clock-ish.'

'Did he give you any indication of where he might go?'

'Said he'd head to London. Some friend had told him where he could get

225

work down there.'

'Well, thank you,' I said, tight-lipped. 'Leo, come on. Leo . . . '

Leo stood stock still for a while, and I knew he was struggling to keep his anger under control. 'You're a disgrace,' he finally said. 'He's your wife's sister's boy, and you turned him away.'

'Yeah, well his mother wasn't worth much, was she? He'll go the same way, you mark my words. By the time he's twenty-five he'll be in prison and even you'll have given up on him.'

'No,' said Leo. 'That's one thing I won't do.' He turned away and I breathed a sigh of relief, but it was too soon. He turned back again. 'I paid you a lot of money to let me take Joe. Remember? At the time you were shouting about how family is all-important and you couldn't possibly let the boy go. Until you found out I was well off. Then it was only a matter of how much you could sell him for. If that boy has any bad influences in his life, it'll come from you, not from his mother. If he ends up in prison, it will have started on this night, when you couldn't even give him a bed until I arrived to take him to safety. You turned him away when he needed help. I never did. Remember that when you're gloating about how you always knew he'd turn into a bad 'un.' Leo pointed his finger in the man's face and for one awful moment I thought he would hit him. 'Remember that.'

The man just glared back at him, too stupid to take it in. If he turned out to be right about Joe, he would never admit his own place in setting the boy on the wrong path.

'Leo, darling,' I said, hardly knowing what I was saying. I was moved by his impassioned speech. 'Come on, he might not have got far. We'll try all the bus stations. We'll try the London road.'

The man sniffed again. 'I er . . . I gave him a couple of bob. For the bus. So I didn't just let him go empty-handed.'

'Oh well,' said Leo bitterly. 'That's all right then.'

We tried the main bus station in

Sheffield, but there was no sign of Joe there. We went to the train station, but no one there had seen him. We had no choice but to try the London road.

The chances of finding him were very slim, but neither of us wanted to give up. We drove until the dawn started to break and we could barely keep our eyes open.

Finally, we found a transport café just before Milton Keynes and called in for a cup of coffee to try and revitalise us. Tired truckers slumped over huge fry-ups, before getting into their cabs and going on their journeys. There were no tacographs in those days, no rules about having a proper break, so many of them drove through the night to their next drop-off, clawing back enough time to get home and be with their families.

The café would be considered sixties chic now, with its Formica-topped tables and chrome-framed chairs. At the time it just looked like a tired old café that was in need of a deep clean. On the ceiling a headache-inducing strip light buzzed and flickered whilst a moth fluttered around it.

Leo ordered beans on toast for two, and whilst we were not really hungry we both ate, as if to fill some other void in our bodies.

'It's impossible,' he said, pushing his empty plate away and rubbing his eyes. 'Once he gets to London, I'll have lost him. I've made such a mess of things, Bobbie. I wanted to give him a stable home life. Then Cindy-Lou turned up and . . . Well, things haven't been easy for any of us. Joe likes you better — and the truth is, so do I.'

'Don't, Leo.'

'Don't what, Bobbie? Don't tell the truth?'

'It makes no difference to the fact that you're married. You have a child.'

'Yes,' he said, gazing out of the window. A ground fog covered the road. 'I can't help thinking,' he said, changing the subject, 'that something must have happened for Joe to run away.'

'He was just a scared kid,' I said. 'But

I don't believe he hurt Mr Rodgers. Unless I really am a bad judge of character.'

'You're not. You're a good judge of character.'

'I'm not so sure,' I said pointedly.

'Oh, you mean me? Well, you did think I was a murderer.'

'The evidence pointed to it, as did your own behaviour as a teenager.'

'Fair enough. But I wasn't.'

'But you are married,' I said, putting my head in my hands. 'And you didn't tell me.'

'Because it was a stupid mistake I made ten years ago that I'd just about forgotten. It was as if I'd dreamed it. I never imagined I'd ever see her again, or that I was still married.'

'We're going around in circles,' I said, sighing heavily. 'The situation is what it is. But that doesn't help us to find Joe.'

We lapsed into silence, looking out the window as Britain began to wake up, and the main road became busier.

'Come out, yer little tike!' a voice

called from across the café some time later. 'Yer can't sleep in there.'

We looked up to see the owner coming out of the gents' loo, pulling someone after him. 'I knew you'd sneak back, yer little . . . '

'Joe!' Leo stood up and crossed the café in an instant. I could hardly believe my eyes, or that finding him would turn out to be so easy. But sometimes things just are. 'Let him go,' Leo said to the owner. 'Let him go now!'

'He was sleeping in my toilets. No doubt planning to rob me when I'd got my back turned.'

'I've got money,' said Joe, taking a pitiful handful of coins out of his pocket. 'I just needed somewhere to sleep.' He looked unkempt, but none the worse for wear.

'Have you eaten?' asked Leo.

'No. I was trying to save my money till I got to London.'

'Get him some breakfast,' Leo commanded the café owner. 'The full works. Bacon, eggs, sausage, beans, toast. And a mug of tea. We'll have more tea too.'

'I don't see why I should . . . '

'Turn down business when your café is empty?' said Leo, looking around at all the empty tables. 'Don't worry, I'll give you a good tip. Just get some food for my brother, please. Come on, Joe.'

'Leo . . . ' Joe started to say.

'No explanations until you've eaten. Come and sit down.'

I got up from my seat and gave Joe a hug. 'We've been so worried about you.'

'I didn't do anything,' Joe said, slumping down into the seat opposite me. 'I like Mr Rodgers. He's a great bloke. I'd never hurt him.'

'Hush now,' said Leo. 'Eat first, talk later.' My heart swelled with love for him, whilst breaking in two at the same time. He made a wonderful big brother to Joe and he would make a wonderful father to Mikey. I had dreamed that one day he would be the father of my children, but that would never happen now.

The café owner came over and

slammed a plate down in front of Joe. Leo and I ordered more tea and a Chelsea bun each, which only made him scowl more. But he was smart enough to realise that Leo was affluent and could pay for any amount of tea and cake.

With the resilience of youth, Joe ate everything on his plate and then asked for cake, which he washed down with his mug of tea. It felt good to see him eat so well. When he had finished, he wiped his mouth and burped. 'Pardon me,' he said, grinning.

'Now, tell us what happened,' I said. 'We've been worried sick about you.'

'I didn't hurt Mr Rodgers. I swear it.'

'Start at the beginning,' Leo said.

'He promised to take me to the pub for a cider when I'd finished his garden at the end of the week,' Joe explained. 'He said it would do him good to get out. So we went, on Saturday night. I did tell you, Leo.'

'Yes, I know. Go on.'

'We went to the pub at eight o'clock

and he ordered a Woodpecker cider for me and a Guinness for himself. But I think he regretted coming out. He was really quiet all night. We had a game of darts, but his heart wasn't in it and I won. So about twenty past nine, he said he wanted to go home. I thought he was tired. We said goodbye at the crossroads — you know, near to Mrs Higgins's caravan — and that was it. I asked if he wanted me to see him back to his house but he said, 'No, lad, you get on home. I've got some thinking to do.''

'That was at nine thirty, Joe,' Leo said. 'You didn't come in till much later.'

'Mr Rodgers gave me a couple of bob to go to the pictures,' said Joe. 'He said he didn't want to spoil my evening. So I went to see Elvis in *Blue Hawaii*. I only caught the last half hour of it anyway. It's not as good as his early films.' I begged to differ, but it was not a time to argue. 'Then I came home.' Joe looked down at the table, picking at the crumbs on his plate.

'I sense you've missed something out there, Joe,' I said, my policewoman's intuition going into overdrive. 'What else happened?' Having a sudden brainwave, I asked, 'Did it have something to do with the break-in at the boarding house?'

Joe's eyes flashed at me, alarmed. 'I didn't steal anything.'

Leo sighed and put his head in his hands. 'Why, Joe? I give you all you need, don't I? Why do you do things like this?'

'I can't say.' Joe clamped his lips shut. 'Because it'll get someone else into trouble.'

'And you can't rat on your mates, right?' I said, raising an eyebrow. 'Where are your mates now, Joe, when you're suspected of beating up an old man? Where are they?'

'It's not like that. It's not other lads,' Joe said vehemently. 'And I didn't hurt Mr Rodgers.' He brushed away tears from his eyes impatiently, looking more like a ten-year-old than a teenager. It was a reminder of just how young he was. 'I wouldn't hurt him. If I tell you, do you promise not to tell anyone else?'

'I can't make that promise, Joe, you know that,' I said.

'But it'll get her into trouble. She's already had to live on the streets.'

'Who has?' I frowned.

'Verity. She's a girl who works at the bank.'

'Yes, I know,' I said. 'I've met her a few times.' I did not tell him in what circumstances.

'Well, she had a row with her boyfriend and he bug . . . he took off and left her alone outside the pictures. She was stranded and had to get back to the boarding house by ten-thirty, otherwise she'd be locked out and lose her place. Her boyfriend had roughed her up a bit. She was in a right state. So I took her to the all-night café and got her a cup of tea, then I walked her back to the boarding house. She was locked out, and she was terrified of admitting to the landlady that she was late, so I erm . . . I helped her to get in. We just broke one little window on the back door, that's all, so we could reach around and unlock it. We didn't take anything. If she'd been caught she would have been on the streets again, and I don't think that rubbish boyfriend would have helped.'

Leo had pulled his hands away from his face as he listened to Joe's story. His face, which had been grim, had relaxed, and had broken into a grin by the end of Joe's story. 'So all this is about you being a knight in shining armour.'

'You told me that you don't leave a girl stranded alone at night, Leo. Remember, it was that night you'd had to take Bobbie home because her Vespa broke down. I was only doing what you'd have done.'

'I hope I wouldn't have broken into someone's house,' said Leo.

'If we tell the cops,' Joe said, looking at me, 'It'll come out about Verity being out late. She'll lose her room in the boarding house then she'll lose her job.'

'I'll sort it out,' I said. I was sure that

when I explained things to Sergeant Simmonds he would be discreet about it for Verity's sake. At least I hoped so. 'But you have to come back, Joe. Running away makes you look guilty.' I turned to Leo. 'How is Mr Rodgers? With everything that's happened, I forgot to ask.'

'He's in intensive care. They were keeping him in a coma, so as to bring down the swelling in his brain.'

'Poor man,' I said. 'So he can't tell us anything about his attacker.'

'No, not yet. We'd better get back,' Leo said. 'We'll drop you off in Scarborough and then head back to Stony End.'

'It's miles out of your way,' I said. 'I'll get a bus back.'

'You will not,' said Leo. 'What was that rule, Joe?'

'You don't leave a girl stranded at night.'

'It's six o'clock in the morning.'

'Same thing. Come on. I'd better pay Attila over there.'

The owner's smile was much wider

by the time he received Leo's tip. 'Lad just having a wild moment, was he, sir?' he asked.

'Something like that,' said Leo.

'Well in my day he'd have got a good hiding, but I suppose you know best. You're his father.'

'I'm his brother, but yes, in this instance I do know best.' Leo's opinion about beating children was written all over his face and I suspected that if he could have taken some of his tip back, he would have.

'You should have come to me when you were in trouble,' Leo said to Joe as he drove us back towards Scarborough. I had offered to drive, but he would not let anyone drive his car, even if he was dog-tired.

'You've got enough to do with Cindy-Lou.' There was some bitterness in Joe's voice.

Leo sighed. 'She's tried really hard with you, Joe.'

Joe harrumphed. 'Yeah, when you're there. When you're not there, it's different. She's told me that if she can arrange for me to stay in boarding school all year, then she will.'

'I don't believe it,' said Leo, but something in his voice told me that he did. 'Anyway, it won't happen. In fact, I was thinking that once you'd done your O-levels, you could go to the local grammar school and finish your A-levels. The only reason I haven't mentioned it before is because I didn't want to interfere with your exams.'

'Really? Stay in Stony End? What will Cindy-Lou say?'

'Cindy-Lou won't be paying the school fees. I will.'

I stared out of the window, feeling completely left out of the conversation as they made their plans for Joe to leave his school and spend more time in Stony End, nearer to the support that only Leo could give him. Their lives had moved on since I left Stony End, and yet it had only been a few weeks. They had their whole future planned. At that moment, I could not see where my future lay at all. I was trapped in a void between the life I had known with Leo and the life I would have to get used to without him.

' . . . your case . . . ' I heard Leo say. 'Bobbie? Have you fallen asleep?'

'What? No. Sorry. Did you say something?'

'I asked you about your case. The one you were investigating about the woman in the castle grounds.'

'We think we might have identified her, though nothing is certain yet.'

'Tell me about it,' he said gently.

'You won't be interested.' Mr Markham's forbidding expression flashed before my eyes.

'I'm pretty sure I will be. I always was, wasn't I? Interested your cases?'

'Yes, of course you were.'

'So tell us. If you can, that is.'

'I'm sure I can, since most of it is an old case. Anyway, I trust you and Joe. It looks as if the killer has killed before. Once in Scarborough then twice in Stony End, just before the war started.

The woman he killed in Scarborough was called Violet Johnson. It was the same M.O.'

'M.O.?' said Joe from the back seat.

'Modus operandi,' I said. 'Method of killing, if you prefer. He strangled her with a Paisley scarf. The man used the name Richard Gloucester. Then, if it's the same man, he was stationed at the air base just outside Stony End, and used the name Harold York. That was when Ruth Yates and Betty Norris were murdered. Harold York was the name of a victim of a bombing along the east coast the Great War, which may be where he got the idea from. But if Mr Rodgers is to be believed, he also used the name George Clarence to forge some cheques. Then, if we're right and the latest victim is Harriet Johnson, she's the daughter of Violet Johnson, and for some reason she packed in her job and went to Stony End, where she was killed. I think that she might have known the killer and either decided to confront him or blackmail him.'

'Why blackmail?' asked Leo.

'She seemed the sort. She'd stolen from her place of work before now, and it was only her resignation that stopped her from getting into more trouble. Her grandmother said that her only response to her mother's death was to wonder how much money was in it for her. I hope I'm wrong and that she just wanted to confront the murderer. Either way that does suggest that he's in Stony End, doesn't it? And that maybe he killed Harriet to stop his secret coming out.'

'Why hasn't anyone recognised him, though?' asked Joe. 'If he was around before the war?'

'It's over twenty years, Joe,' I said. 'He was a young man then. Maybe in his twenties, I don't know. He'd be older now. Maybe a bit heavier, a bit balder, a bit fatter. Who knows? And he wasn't a part of the community. He was stationed at the airbase so he wouldn't have come into town very often. Maybe just at night, and then he seemed to keep to the less salubrious areas of Stony End. Only someone like Mr Rodgers, who was stationed there with him, would have remembered and . . . ' I stopped. 'Oh God . . . '

'Mr Rodgers saw him,' said Leo in a flat voice. 'On Saturday night when he was out with Joe. That's why he was attacked.'

'We don't know that,' I said, trying to remain impartial. But the idea began to take hold. 'It could have been the lads — the other lads — who were victimising him a few months ago. But it makes more sense, doesn't it, that Mr Rodgers could have seen him somewhere that night. Which means . . . '

'Mr Rodgers is still in danger,' said Joe. 'We've got to go and help him.' His young face was alight with the drama and I sensed he could see himself as Mr Rodgers's saviour. I smiled, remembering my own hopes to be a heroine when I first joined the police force.

'First we have to get Bobbie back home,' said Leo. 'We're not far from

Scarborough now.' The morning had broken into a day of supreme sunshine. It would be busy on the beach as day-trippers piled in to make the most of the weather.

'I'll telephone the sarge and put the idea to him,' said Bobbie. 'Hopefully he'll listen and make sure Mr Rodgers is safe. Joe, can you remember who you saw when you and Mr Rodgers were out?'

'Well, everyone. It was Saturday night in Stony End, so people were going to the pub and the working men's club. A few of them spoke to us. The sarge, Alf Norris and his wife, Mrs Higgins, Reg the wino.'

'Joe!' Leo admonished.

I laughed. 'I'm surprised that man is still alive,' I said. 'He was one of the first people I met when I moved to Stony End last year. He thought the idea of a woman police officer was hilarious.'

'I was the first person you met,' said Leo.

'Well sort of, along with Annabel. She'd forgotten to put her handbrake on and her car ran away and I ran after it, thinking I was a Hollywood stuntman!' I laughed again. 'Oh God, remember that, Leo? And I put a dent in your car. Ouch.'

'It recovered,' said Leo, smiling. 'I'm not sure I ever did though.'

'Nor me,' I whispered.

Leo pulled up outside the Markhams' house. 'Do you want us to wait?' he said. 'To help you to explain?'

'Explain what? I'm a grown woman. Go on, get back to Stony End. You're going to be exhausted as it is.'

I hesitated, wondering if I should kiss him on the cheek. Wasn't that what friends did when they parted? Only I was not sure Leo and I could ever be friends. Not in a platonic way. Too much had happened between us. 'Take care,' I whispered, and got out of the car.

I watched as Leo drove off, determined not to let him see how nervous I really was about returning to the Markhams' house after being out all night. My heart ached, and even though I knew I would probably see Leo again, it still felt like an ending as they drove off to make plans in which I had no part.

17

It was very quiet when I went in, and for a moment I wondered if they were still in bed, but by then it was mid-morning and Mr Markham did not hold with lie-ins, as I had found out on my first day off soon after moving in with them.

I crept upstairs and was about to go into my room when the door to the Markhams' room opened with a bang. 'What time do you call this?' said Mr Markham, looming over me.

'I call it Charlie. What do you call it?' I said, immediately regretting it. He was not a man to whom one should make jokes.

'How dare you bring this house into disrepute? I told Enid when you moved in that you'd be trouble. Oh don't think I don't know about you, young lady, with your Italian lover and your other married boyfriend. That was him in the car, wasn't it? I daresay that was his bastard son with him.' I wondered how he could know any of this.

'Well, you say wrong,' I retorted, anger rising. 'Joe is Leo's half-brother and he'd run away, so I went with Leo to help him to find him. That's the only reason I've been out all night. To help a child in trouble.'

'So you say. But I know your sort.'

'I shan't ask how,' I said, pointedly. 'I don't care if you believe me or not, Mr Markham. But you have no right to lecture me. You're not my father.'

'I am your landlord.'

'Actually no, you're not. The constabulary are my landlords, just as they're yours.' I knew I was being rude. After all, it was Markham's home even if he didn't own it, but his attitude infuriated me. I could not help but compare it with Leo's supportive behaviour over my career. If Markham had even tried to understand, I would not have been so angry, but weeks of him talking down to me and treating my career as if it meant nothing had finally pushed me over the edge. I was also dog-tired from lack of sleep and not in the mood for any more of his ranting.

'You will leave here today. I've already told Enid to report you to your superiors. I'm sure they don't want you bringing the good name of the constabulary down. But you won't stay another night in this house.'

'Well, thank God for that,' I said, glaring at him. At a bare five feet four inches, I was several inches shorter than him, but I stood as tall as I could. 'Because you are a brute. You have an intelligent, hardworking wife and you treat her like dirt. Well you don't get to treat me the same way.'

The next thing I knew, Markham had raised his hand and I could almost feel the slap he intended to give me.

'Just try it,' I hissed between my teeth. 'Just once. It will be the very last thing you do. Because I will report you to the police and I will stand up in court and tell everyone what a bully you are.'

'You need a good slap, my girl.' Nevertheless he lowered his hand. I felt relief wash over me.

'So do you,' said a voice from the stairs. I turned to see Leo standing there. 'Would you like me to show you how it feels when someone bigger than you raises their hand to you, Mr Markham?'

'Who the hell are you?'

'I'm her married lover. Remember? The one she's been out all night with. You thought you just saw me driving away in the car, but I had a feeling I'd be needed so I stopped around the corner and came back. Come on, Bobbie. Get your things. You're not staying in this house another day.'

Leo waited outside my bedroom door whilst I threw all my clothes into a suitcase. Mr Markham had gone downstairs to the sitting room, and I could almost hear him seething. It said a lot that he had backed down completely in front of Leo. But it annoyed me too.

'I didn't need you to rescue me,' I told Leo as he carried my suitcase downstairs.

'You're welcome,' he said. We walked down the path and out of the garden.

'Oh, but it's not fair, Leo. I should be able to take care of myself, yet if you hadn't come I don't know what would have happened . . . ' I burst into tears. Leo dropped the suitcase and put his arms around me. 'I want to be a strong and capable woman, but these weeks in this awful house with that man have turned me into a wimp. I can only guess how his poor wife feels.'

'Shh,' said Leo, holding me close. It felt so good, but also wicked. And that also felt good in ways it should not have. 'You don't have to go back there. Come home.'

'I do have to stay here, Leo. Not here, in this house, but I can't leave Scarborough. I am still supposed to finish up my stint here, even if that ends today. You and Joe need to get back. I haven't even had a chance to call the sarge and warn him about Mr Rodgers.'

'We're going to book into a hotel overnight. Joe is exhausted and so am I. Come on, I'll book you a room too.'

'I know where we can stay,' I said, giving in through sheer exhaustion.

Half an hour later, we had rooms in Mrs Brown's Bed and Breakfast. I had deliberately chosen her, knowing her strict policy on unmarried couples sharing. I did not want any temptation where Leo was concerned.

'You're lucky,' said Mrs Brown, giving Leo an appreciative glance. 'We've got two rooms left. One is a twin, the other a double. Now who will be sharing with who?'

'I'll share the twin room with my brother,' said Leo. 'Let Bobbie have the double room.'

Leo and Joe went straight to bed to get some sleep, but I had to go into the station so I dropped my suitcase in the pretty double room and went out.

As soon as I reached the station, Sergeant Markham called me to her office. Her face was grim and I got the impression she did not like me much at that moment. I sat down and waited for a telling-off.

'My husband has explained what happened,' she said through gritted teeth.

'Everything?' I raised an eyebrow. 'Like him raising his hand to me?'

She faltered for a moment, but continued to speak quietly but firmly. 'Did it not occur to you, Blandford, that as a guest in our home, it might have been polite to let us know where you were taking off to? Did it not occur to you that I might have lain awake and worried about you? I am responsible for you whilst you're here, after all.'

'No, it didn't occur to me to say anything.' I lowered my head in shame, finally accepting that I had behaved badly. My excuse was that Mr Markham had riled me so much that I did not think he deserved any explanation about my whereabouts.

Sergeant Markham was different. Though stern at times, she had shown me nothing but kindness. 'I'm sorry. It's just that everything happened so quickly. I was worried about Joe and . . . ' I could not explain the rest. How Leo being there had unsettled me. I was not sure she would understand that type of love. I finally had the courage to look her in the eyes. 'I am sorry for any problems I might have caused you, Sergeant Markham. Truly I am.'

Her eyes flickered, then returned to flint-hard blackness. 'Where are you staying now?'

'At Mrs Brown's guest house. Steve Brown's grandmother.'

'Oh yes, I know of her. I think that under the circumstances you'd best stay there till the end of the week, and then I'll find an excuse to send you back to Stony End. There's no need to put a mark on your record.'

No, I thought, because your husband was going to hit me and you know it. You also know I could make a big thing of it if I wanted to. Truth be known, I did not want to. It was easy for me, because I could walk away, but Sergeant Markham still had to live with the man. Whether I thought she should put up with it was another matter. It was her choice to make, not mine. 'Thank you, Sergeant Markham,' I muttered.

'Good. You may leave.'

'Sergeant?' I said as I reached the door.

'Yes, Blandford?'

'I just wanted to say that we get lots of women in the station, both here and at Stony End, who have . . . problems . . . at home. Sometimes I think it would be good if we took our own advice.' I looked at her for a long time to see if she got my meaning, but her expression remained inscrutable.

'Thank you, Blandford. That will be all.'

I left her and then sighed impatiently. I had wanted to find out how Mr Markham had learned so much about me, but there had been no opportunity. I went down to the canteen for a cup of tea, hoping it would keep me going a while. I had been awake over twenty-four hours and it was starting to take its toll.

The first thing I saw was the inspector's stripes, so I immediately saluted. Then I saw the man they belonged to. Inspector Kirkham. And standing next to him was PC Porter. Then I knew how Mr Markham had found out about me. Kirkham and Porter had made my life in Stony End very difficult in my first year of probation, and it seemed they were determined to keep doing that.

'Well, if it isn't WPC Blandford,' said Kirkham, his lips curling.

'Sir,' I said, nodding my head curtly. 'What brings you to Scarborough?'

'Porter and I are simply doing some cross-departmental diplomacy. Visiting the other stations to see how they're getting on, and whether we can learn something from each other.'

I wanted to laugh at that, but thought better of it. Odd how I could stand up to Mr Markham, yet these two men reduced me to a silent wreck. I still held the memory of them trying to ink-stamp my chest as a form of initiation.

'Well, it's nice to see you, sir,' I said, even though it was anything but. 'I'd better get on.'

'So had we.' The inspector leered, then brushed past me. Porter went to follow him, but paused when he was abreast of me. 'Did Steve Brown win his bet yet?' he asked.

'What bet?'

'To see if he could get you into bed. I heard the lads talking about it.'

Strangely the truth meant nothing to me. I was not in love with Steve Brown so I did not care what he had done or not done. I admit I was a little disappointed in him, but my own instincts had already told me he was not to be trusted. 'Well then you should know the answer,' I said.

'It's hard to tell with you, Blandford. You look as pure as the driven snow, but there's a lot happened in your past.'

'You mean like the day you tried to stamp me as vermin?' I hissed, glaring at him. 'You'd better go, Porter. The inspector might be forced to open his own car door and I'm sure you wouldn't want that.'

His spotty face flushed scarlet. 'I'm very important in the inspector's team.'

'Of course you are. Especially since no other station will have you now.'

Porter stared at me and I could see him trying to work out what to say. But he had never been very clever. Still, when he had gone I let out a huge sigh of relief. He may not be clever, but the inspector was, and between them they could ruin my career.

I certainly knew how to pick my enemies. Kirkham, Porter, Markham. All the type of man who hated intelligent and successful women, and who did all they could to stop our progression. Nowadays I could probably take them to a tribunal and they would be forced to face up to their behaviour. But nineteen sixty-one was still very much a man's world, and those men ruled it with a rod of iron. Kirkham and Porter could play havoc with my career in both Scarborough and Stony End; and Markham, whilst having no power in the police force, had a lot of influence over his wife, who also had the power to make things difficult for me. Somehow I doubted Sergeant Markham would. She was afraid of her husband, but she was also a professional when it came to her job.

My hands were shaking as I drank my tea, both with tiredness and the stress of the encounters. I wished I could run away again, to somewhere else. I could not bear the thought of going back to Stony End and having to face Leo and his wife. But neither did I want to stay in Scarborough.

Steve Brown came into the canteen

as I was finishing my tea. He smiled warmly, but I believed I could see behind that now. He was just like his grandmother's Pyrex crockery. Smooth and glossy, but with hidden chips that would cut you to bits.

'How are you, Bobbie?'

'I'm very well, thank you, Steve.' I debated whether to say anything about the bet, but decided against it. I was not in the mood for another confrontation. I had paperwork to complete and then I hoped I could go and get some much-needed sleep.

'Gran says you're staying with us.'

'I'm staying at the guest house, yes.'

'Great! The more the merrier. How about we go to the pictures tonight?'

'No, thank you. I have other plans.' Sleep being the main one. I got up from my table and left, aware of Steve's eyes following me. He would wonder what had gone wrong, but I did not care. I was done with men, both romantically and as colleagues. When I returned to Stony End I would ask Sergeant

Simmonds for a transfer elsewhere. Somewhere far away from all the men who were, at that moment, the bane of my life.

Even Leo? a small voice inside me asked. *Especially Leo*, I replied silently. The sooner he was gone from my life, the better.

★ ★ ★

With everything that had happened, I realised I still had not telephoned Sergeant Simmonds in Stony End to warn him about Mr Rodgers. I went to a phone box, not wanting anyone to hear what I had to say. I also filled the sarge in on what I knew so far about the aliases used by the man who I thought was the killer.

'York, Clarence, Gloucester. It sounds like the Wars of the Roses, Blandford,' said the Sarge. His words were like striking a match in my head, but before I could see what it illuminated, the flame went out and it was lost to me. 'Thank you for warning me about Mr Rodgers,' the sarge continued. 'We'll keep a good eye on him. But I do have some sad news for you.'

'What's that?'

'Mrs Atkins died yesterday.'

'Was she murdered?' I asked, my mind full of the images of stricken women and the evil that men did.

'No, Blandford. She was just old and tired. But she left you a note. We're not allowed to open it, so the sooner you come back here, the better.'

'It'll be very soon, Sarge.' I hesitated.

'What's happened, Blandford?'

'I'm afraid I may have brought the service into disrepute,' I said. Ridiculously, I began to cry and I hated crying in front of the Sarge. I always wanted to prove I was as tough as the men under his command. I sniffed loudly and held back the tears as much as I could.

'And how might you have done that?'

'I erm . . . went with Leo to look for Joe and we stayed out all night. Mr Markham was not very happy. But he was going to hit me, Sarge, and nothing justifies that.'

'I see.' The sarge could be very closed when he wanted to be and I longed to know what he was really thinking. 'I see.'

'Sergeant Markham is going to request that I leave Scarborough early. I'll be leaving in disgrace, even if she covers it up, Sarge. I'm so sorry to have let you down.'

'We'll talk about it when you return, Blandford.'

'Inspector Kirkham and Peter Porter have been here too, spreading gossip about me.'

'I heard he was in the area,' said the sarge in noncommittal tones. 'Is there anything else I need to know?'

I almost told him about Steve Brown's bet, but that was too embarrassing and it had nothing much to do with the case or my standing in the Scarborough police force. 'No, Sarge. Leo — Doctor Stanhope — will be bringing Joe back to answer questions very soon.'

'Yes, I know. He already telephoned me to that effect. Give me the number of that hotel you're staying at, as I may want to contact you,' he said.

I did as he asked, and we said our goodbyes. I really felt like crying then. It was stupid, but I even missed the sarge. He could be abrupt and grumpy at times, but he was a good man underneath it all.

As I walked back to the hotel, I worried about my future. I was still on probation, and the sarge could easily decide to let me go rather than risk me embarrassing the police force. It had not occurred to me to be anything but honest to him, as he had a way of finding things out. He had saved my bacon more than once during my probationary period. I could not assume he would always be willing to do so. Especially if I kept getting myself into trouble.

When I got back to the hotel, Leo was alone in the residents' lounge. I went in and fell into his arms. Yes, I know I had decided to have nothing more to do with him, but he was a familiar face in what I saw as a strange and hostile environment. Plus, his arms felt good around me, as if they belonged there.

'Hey,' he whispered. 'Come on now. This is not like you.'

'I've made such a mess of things,' I said. 'I don't think they'll let me stay in the force anymore, Leo. I should have told Sergeant Markham where I was going. But her husband made me so mad, the way he bullied us both, that I forgot my manners. I told the sarge about it, but I don't know what he thinks.'

Leo put me away from him a little, but didn't let me go. Then he used one hand to brush my hair back, and then wipe a stray tear from my cheeks. 'It won't be the end of the world, Bobbie, even if it feels that way. You're young, intelligent and hard-working. You'll find something else.'

'I don't want something else, Leo. I want this. I want to wear this uniform and help people. I want to find justice for those poor women who died at the hands of this Wars of the Roses killer.'

'Wars of the Roses?'

'The sarge said the names sounded like the Wars of the Roses. York, Gloucester, Clarence.'

That was when it hit me. The thing that had been hiding in the dark. I gasped. 'Oh my God. We've been so blind. I've been so blind.' I pulled away from Leo and paced the room. 'Can it really be that easy though? I have to get back to Stony End, Leo. Now.'

18

Despite my dramatic words, I could not just leave Scarborough. There were procedures to go through before I left the station. So Leo managed to talk me down and persuaded me to get some sleep. I thought it would be impossible, with so much going through my mind. It was ten o'clock in the evening when there was a knock on my door.

'The telephone for you, Bobbie,' said Mrs Brown. 'It's rather late, dear.' I sensed she was struggling to be nice to me because I was Steve's friend and that if I had been any other young woman taking calls at night, she would have shown her disapproval more willingly.

'I'm coming,' I said sleepily. It took me a few minutes to get my bearings and wake up enough to go to the hallway where the telephone was kept. I expected it to be Sergeant Simmonds, as he was the only one I had given the number to, but it was Sergeant Markham.

'There has been a special request made,' she said without ceremony. 'Sergeant Simmonds has said that he can't manage without you much longer, so you're to return to Stony End tomorrow.'

'Oh.' My heart lifted. I was going home! The feeling was momentary. I did not know what I was returning to. 'I see.'

'Under the circumstances, since you've been recalled,' said Sergeant Markham, 'I've decided it would be unpolitic to mention the recent problems. I've no wish to destroy the career of a young policewoman. So we'll say no more about what has happened, and I will just wish you well for the future.' I wondered exactly what the sarge had said to her. I suspected that he pointed out that things could be rather embarrassing for her if I decided to make an issue of her husband's behaviour, but I never did find out exactly what passed between them.

'Thank you, Sergeant Markham,' I said. 'Thank you so much. I hope . . . I hope you'll be all right.'

'I will be perfectly all right, thank you, WPC Blandford.'

There was little else I could say. It is probably hard for women in the twenty-first century to understand why an intelligent woman like Sergeant Markham would stay with such a man. But women of her era believed that marriage was for life, and no matter how bad things got, she would not be persuaded otherwise. No amount of wishing on my part would change things. I could only use her experience as a guide for my own life and hope that I would not make the same mistakes.

I put the telephone back in its cradle and turned to see Steve watching me. Feeling exposed wearing just my nightclothes, I pulled my dressing gown around me. 'Hello,' I said as cheerily as possible. 'I hope I didn't disturb you.'

'You always disturb me, Bobbie. You've been disturbing me since you arrived.'

'Well, I can only apologise.' I made to get past him, but he blocked my way. 'I'm very tired, and I have to leave early in the morning.' I wanted to ask Leo if I could travel back with him and Joe.

Steve put his hands on my shoulders. 'I really like you, Bobbie.'

'Steve, please don't. I . . . I don't feel that way about you, and even if I did, I wouldn't . . . ' I hesitated.

'Wouldn't what?'

'I wouldn't want to be the subject of someone's bet, all right?' I put my hands on my hips and tried to stand tall, though I felt oppressed by his hands on my shoulders.

'Bobbie, the bet means nothing. That's just the lads having a laugh. I never really intended to try to win it.'

'So what are you doing now? I presume you've just heard that I'm due to leave in the morning. Maybe you think this is your last chance? Well, you never had a chance, Steve. I'm sorry, but that's the way it is.'

'What?' he said, his lips curling, making him look remarkably unattractive. 'Am I not married enough for you?'

'How dare you?' I whispered, my cheeks flaming red. 'Let go of me.'

Where was Leo when I needed him? Why did he not rush in and save me? I felt more threatened with Steve than I had with Mr Markham, but it was a different type of threat. 'Let me go, Steve, and we'll say nothing more about this.'

'You're not going to make a fool of me, Bobbie. Not with the lads.'

'So it *is* about the bet?'

'Not just that. It's about pride as well. You're not letting me go back to them with my tail between my legs.'

The double entendre, which I don't think he really intended, only made me want to laugh. 'Well you're not putting it anywhere else,' I said, and started giggling. It was probably the cruellest thing I could have done to him, but at least I did not feel intimidated anymore. 'Let go of me, Steve. Now. Before I call your grandmother.'

That had the desired effect. His hands dropped to his sides. 'Bobbie,' he said, looking shamefaced, 'I didn't mean . . . I wouldn't have . . . '

'Goodbye, Steve,' I said, brushing past him and running up the stairs. I ran into my room and locked the door, then put a chair under the handle just in case. I would have to speak to Leo in the morning.

A few seconds later there was a knock on my door. 'You okay, Bobbie?' It was Leo.

'Yes, I'm fine,' I said, irrationally annoyed with him for not being there when I needed him.

'Good. He won't bother you again, I promise. He certainly won't be winning any bets for a while.'

I pressed my head against the door. He had been there, somewhere, listening to it all. He had stayed out of the way because he thought that was what I had wanted. 'Thank you,' I whispered. 'Leo . . .'

'Yes?'

'Can I travel back with you tomorrow?'

'I'm certainly not letting you go back to Stony End alone. Get some sleep. We'll leave early in the morning.'

I kissed the door at the spot where I thought his lips might be. My love for him swelled in my chest, along with the pain of knowing he would never be mine again. He was still married with a child, and we'd never be able to be together; but he cared about me and, more importantly, he respected me despite the mistakes I had made in my past. I did not know if we could survive as friends in the future, but at that moment he was my very best friend. 'Thank you.'

At breakfast the following morning, Mrs Brown was decidedly frosty. Steve popped in to get some toast, but seemed unable to sit down comfortably.

I suppressed a grin and saw Leo do the same. Joe was oblivious to it all. He looked out of the window with a pensive expression on his face.

'It will be all right, Joe,' said Leo. 'I promise.'

Joe just nodded, but I must admit I was terrified he would do a runner again. He was young and overwhelmed by the situation in which he found himself. Heck, I had run away myself when things got too bad in Stony End, so I was in no position to judge him.

When Leo and Joe had finished their breakfast, they excused themselves so they could go and finish their packing. At some point the day before, Leo had bought Joe some new clothes to wear and a bag in which to carry his old clothes.

I sipped my tea, apprehensive about returning to Stony End, but also happy. I would be seeing my friend, Annabel, and all the other people who made Stony End so special to me — Alf and Greta Norris, Mrs Higgins, and even the sarge, though I would never have admitted that to him! And I would be close to Leo. I did not know how long I could stand that, with his wife and child in such close proximity, but for that moment I decided to just go with the flow and see where life took me. All I knew was that it would be a long time before I wanted to set foot in Scarborough again.

I heard a loud sniff behind me and turned to see Mrs Brown clearing the tables. All the other residents had gone out for the day and would not be returning until dinner-time. That was the rule of the house.

'Are you all right, Mrs Brown?' I asked.

'I reckon,' she said, slamming a salt pot down onto the table. 'It's . . . well, it's just that you think a person is nice and then . . . I'm very disappointed in you, Bobbie, very, and all I can say is that my Steve has had a lucky break.'

I wanted to tell her about the bet, but for some reason decided against it. Let her keep her delusions about her grandson. A lot of his attitude to women came from her, so I doubted it would make a lot of difference anyway.

'Yes, I agree,' I said, standing up.

Mrs Brown raised an eyebrow. 'Oh do you, now?'

'Yes. He'd never have been able to handle me.'

'Well, I . . . I'm sure I've never heard anything like that.'

'Mrs Brown,' I said, lowering my voice. 'I know that your daughter had an illegitimate child. So please don't judge me.'

'Not with a married man, she didn't,' she retorted.

Well, she had me there, but I was not about to be made to feel small by such a small-minded woman. 'Leo and I are not lovers, whatever you may think. I respect the fact he is married and has a child and I won't help him to break his vows.'

'What about the other one? The Russian?'

I almost laughed then. 'He was Italian, and I didn't know he was married. As soon as I found out, I ended the relationship. Have you never made a mistake, Mrs Brown?' According to Mrs Johnson, she had, but she would never admit it.

'I've lived a good Christian life.'

'Good for you,' I said, tired of her sanctimony. Where was the warm and welcoming woman I had met only a couple of days earlier? Then, I supposed, she had seen me as a potential girlfriend for her grandson, and Steve had probably not told her what else he knew about me until the previous evening when he had failed to win his bet. I don't know about hell having no fury like a woman scorned. A man was perfectly capable of destroying a woman's reputation just because she had turned him down. Especially in a society where female morality was held as an impossible ideal.

I would like to say that I said something pithy to Mrs Brown that made her see life differently. Something that made her change her attitude towards her fellow woman and regret that she had brought her grandson up with the same mindset. Sadly real life is not like that. People can seldom be made to alter their deep-seated prejudices, least of all by a few well-chosen words from someone for whom they have little or no respect.

'Mrs Brown,' I said, changing the subject, 'I wondered if before I left I might have a look at the picture of your South American cousins again.'

'Why?' She looked afraid and it was then I realised that she knew. Or at least she had suspected something for a long time.

'It's pertinent to my investigation. I could get my colleagues to come around with a warrant,' I said.

That did the trick. Whilst it gave her kudos to have a grandson in the police force, she would not want a bunch of officers turning up at her door. 'There's no need,' she sniffed. 'You can see it.

I've nothing to hide. I'm not sure what you expect to find out.'

Five minutes later I had the picture in my hand. It was not as conclusive as I had hoped, but it was a starting point.

'I think I've found the killer,' I told Leo as we set off for Stony End.

19

A lump came to my throat as we arrived in Stony End several hours later. It felt like I had been gone for years, yet it also felt like I had been gone for just a few seconds.

It was market day and the streets were bustling. Or as bustling as they ever were in Stony End. A group of men stood in the entrance of the pub, making the most of the all-day opening times, which were reserved for market days only.

Brightly coloured stalls sold house-wares and produce. I waved to Mrs Higgins, who was on one of the stalls selling her homemade chutneys, jams and cakes. Wearing a daffodil-yellow dress with purple pedal pushers and black wellingtons, I was glad to see her sense of style had not changed in my absence. She was so surprised to see me, she almost dropped the jar in her hand. As we passed by I saw her wipe her hands on her dress and say something to her customers.

'Where shall I drop you?' asked Leo. 'At Annabel's, or the station?'

'I should go the station first,' I said. 'You need to go there first.' I looked over my shoulder at Joe, who did not seem as happy to return as I was. 'It'll be all right,' I told him, not for the first time since we set out.

We pulled up at the station. 'Leave your suitcase in the car,' said Leo. 'I'll drop it off for you on our way home.'

'Thanks,' I said, not sure what to say to him now. Returning to Stony End was also returning to the reality of our situation. 'And for the lift. You . . . you're a good friend, Leo.'

'I try to be.'

As we walked up the path to the station, the sarge was coming out. With him was a man I had never seen before, but whom I immediately pegged as American. It was odd how I knew, even

282

though he wasn't wearing cowboy boots and a Stetson. It was in the way he held himself.

'Ah, here is Doctor Stanhope,' said the sarge. 'Doctor, this is Mr Johnson. He's been looking for you for a day or two.'

'Mr Johnson,' said Leo, grinning widely and holding his hand out. 'I hope you have news for me.'

'Yes indeed, Doctor Stanhope. Is there anywhere we can talk in private?'

'We'll go to my car. Joe — ' Leo turned to his brother. ' — stay with Bobbie, and then I'll come in and sort everything out.'

'There's nothing to sort out,' said the sarge. 'Joe is not in any trouble. Mr Rodgers woke up this morning and his first words to the constable were that Joe didn't do it.'

I saw the strain fall from Joe like a sudden fall of rain. Then the sun came out and he was smiling. 'May I go up and see him? Leo, is that okay?'

'Yes, of course, Joe. Here, take some

money for a magazine and some grapes. But not a top-shelf magazine, all right?' Leo winked. 'Mr Rodgers is a poorly man. Thanks, Sergeant Simmonds.'

'There is,' the sarge interrupted, 'the small matter of breaking into the boarding house.'

'Oh . . . ' The sun went in again and Joe looked like a man condemned.

'But that has been explained to us as well,' the sarge continued. 'Pay for the damage, Doctor Stanhope, and we'll say no more about it.'

'Agreed. Go on, Joe. Go and see your pal.'

'What about Verity?' asked Joe.

'She'll be all right, lad,' said the sarge. 'I've explained the situation to the landlady and she agrees that the girl was in a bad situation.'

'Did Mr Rodgers say anything else?' I asked the sarge when Joe and Leo had gone about their business.

'He doesn't know who attacked him, but he has a good idea. He seems to think it's some man called — '

'Harold York?' I offered.

'Yes, Harold York. Now if we could just find him. Mr Rodgers can't remember much about what else happened that night. The doctors say he will, but the blow to the head will take time to heal.'

'I think I know who Harold York is,' I said. 'But we need Mr Rodgers to be able to make a positive identification. We also need to do a bit more digging.'

'Running this case, are you, Blandford?'

'Erm, no, Sarge. Sorry. I just meant . . . '

'Go on,' he said, gesturing to the station. 'Write your report, then tell me all about it.'

'Thank you, Sarge.' I walked towards the door, the thrill of the chase invigorating me.

'Welcome back, Blandford.'

I turned and gave him my brightest smile. 'Thanks, Sarge!'

Things moved slowly in Stony End in the early sixties. We did not have emails, mobile phones or the internet. We did not even have a fax machine at the station. I had been back a few days and was still waiting for confirmation from the RAF that a certain Harold York had been with them during the war. The most I could hope for was a photograph to back up my theory. But the people we liaised with were in no real hurry to provide information from over twenty years before. They had their red tape, just as we had ours.

I did have Mrs Atkins's letter, but that only hinted at who our main suspect was. She had written in a spidery hand:

'Dear WPC Blandford,

I wanted to write to you before my memory went altogether. I can see some things so clearly, whilst others are hazy. I have begun to wonder what it was that made me think so much about that lost bicycle. Now I know it was him, when he came with a delivery for the fête.

I cannot say I recognised him

completely. He was much older than when I last saw him, and has put on some weight. But I knew then that he was the one who had taken my bicycle, because I had seen him standing on the street when I had gone in to deliver the baby.

I am afraid I do not know his name, and I don't think I ever did. I just know that he has returned to Stony End and that something about him troubles me. I hope that this information helps you, as scant as it is.

Your friend,
Elsie Atkins'

I was sad to think that I had not seen her before she died. I never did explain to her that her bicycle might have been used to flee the scene of a crime, but judging by her note Mrs Atkins had been a perceptive woman, and she knew that there was something wrong about the theft and the thief.

Leo had disappeared from my life

again, and I had not seen him since our return to Stony End. I presumed he was getting on with his marriage.

'He hasn't been at the hospital either, sweetie,' Annabel told me over supper one night. 'Nor in his surgery.'

We munched on cheese on toast, and I revelled in the fact that even though it was way past seven o'clock, I was allowed to eat something. 'Perhaps he's gone to America to see his son now that Joe has gone back to boarding school to finish his O-levels,' I said as pain seared through me. 'It's probably just as well. I was going to . . . you know . . . ' I confided in Annabel. 'I had decided not to care about his wife because he obviously doesn't love her. But being back in Stony End has brought me back down to earth. I think my decision to have an affair with him was mostly because of how restricted I felt in Scarborough, surrounded by judgemental people. I worry more about offending the people in Stony End, because everyone has been so good to me.'

'Thank goodness for that,' Annabel said kindly. 'You're not cut out for that sort of intrigue, darling girl. And if you hadn't had a nervous breakdown, I would have. I'm not good at keeping secrets!'

Later that week two things happened to shake the equilibrium of Stony End. First of all the news went out that Mr Rodgers had died overnight. I was glad that Joe was not there to hear about it.

Secondly, Dottie Riley returned, and she was not alone. 'Mum!' I said, wide-eyed, when I answered the front door to them both.

My mum stood on the doorstep, looking contrite. Her red hair was swept into a beehive, and she wore her best suit. 'Hello, sweetheart,' she said. 'I owe you an apology.'

I let them into the cottage and offered them tea, still unable to comprehend that my mother was actually there. When I brought the tea through, Elvis came in from the kitchen and took a sniff at Dottie, then walked out again.

'He's mad at me,' Dottie said, wiping her eyes.

'Well you did run off and leave him,' I chided.

'Dottie was in trouble,' Mum explained, 'and she asked if she could stay with me for a while. That's who was there when you phoned, and that's why I couldn't let you come home when you needed to.'

I sipped my tea, the pain of betrayal still raw. There might not be a boy-friend, but I had needed my mother and she had preferred to help a woman whom she had not seen for nearly twenty years.

'But she was afraid to tell anyone why,' Mum continued when I didn't reply. 'Only, Jack — Sergeant Simmonds — guessed, and now he's ordered her back.'

'I was so afraid,' said Dottie. 'Really I was. I mean I wasn't like them, so I didn't know why he would be interested in me.'

'You weren't like who?' I asked, frowning.

'Those women who were strangled. Ruth Yates and Betty Norris. Well everyone knew they were good-time girls. But I'm not. Yet he came after me.'

'Who came after you?'

'Harold York. I was a married woman then.' I suspected there was more that she was not telling me. I did not care if she had an affair. I just wanted the truth. 'He tried to strangle me with this Paisley scarf he bought me. Ugly old thing it was.' Only Dottie Riley would complain more about a scarf than being strangled. 'I managed to get away, thankfully.'

'And you never told anyone?'

'How could I?' Dottie asked. 'I was married. I didn't want people to think that I . . . well, you know.'

'Women died,' I said indignantly. 'Innocent women.'

'Well . . . ' Dottie said, her face a mask of disapproval.

'Innocent women,' I repeated emphatically. 'But that still doesn't explain why you disappeared several months ago.'

'Well he's back, isn't he? I saw him that day and I was terrified. What if he'd come back to kill me?' Dottie put her hand to her neck, as if she could feel the scarf tightening as we spoke.

'He has killed someone,' I said. 'You know that, don't you? Harriet Johnson. They found her in the castle grounds.' I almost said that if Dottie had told us about him, Harriet Johnson might still be alive, but I was not quite that cruel.

'I was afraid and ashamed,' said Dottie, her eyes filling with tears. 'What would people say?'

'They'd have said you were very brave for coming forward,' I said.

'Well, she's here now,' said my mum. 'And she wants to help, don't you, Dottie?'

'We've already got help,' I sighed. 'But I suppose one more identification won't do any harm. I have to get ready for work, and then you can come with me to the station. I'll arrange a line-up.'

I was up in my room, dressing, when

Mum came in. 'I am sorry, Bobbie.'

'I needed you, Mum, and you weren't there for me. Honestly, you haven't seen Dottie Riley since Dad died. Why was she more important than me?'

'She's wasn't. She's not.' Mum sighed. 'She put me in an impossible situation, Bobbie. Turning up the way she did. She was hysterical. I know you're angry with her, but she's a lonely woman in her fifties. Her reputation is all she has now.' She came over to me and stroked my hair back. 'You never could get that hair under control, could you? Let me help you.'

'I can do it myself,' I said, turning away. 'I needed you, Mum.'

'The truth is, you haven't needed me for a long time, Bobbie. You shut me out. You hardly ever talk about your life here. I didn't think you needed me anymore.'

'I thought you disapproved of me being in the force,' I said. 'That's why I don't tell you much about it.'

'I admit I was against it at first, but Jack Simmonds tells me you're doing splendidly. I am proud of you and I do want to know about your life.'

'I'm a mess,' I said, tears falling down my cheeks. 'I've made the same mistake twice, Mum. Falling in love with a married man. When will I ever learn?'

She stood behind me and put her hands on my shoulders. 'Maybe soon. Maybe never. People don't always, sweetheart. But that doesn't make you a bad person. Isn't that what you were trying to tell Dottie about the two other women who died?'

I turned and let her take me in her arms. This was what I had wanted for months. The love of my mother. 'Thanks for not judging me, Mum.'

'I'm not Dottie Riley,' Mum whispered. 'I must admit, I shan't be sorry when she's back in her chip shop, even though she does a smashing Friday night supper.'

I laughed through my tears. 'We'll be glad too. Her sister is a lousy cook.'

'Are we all set?' asked the sarge. 'The line-up is ready.'

Dottie Riley, who was sitting in one of the back rooms with a cup of tea, looked as if she might make a run for it, but her fear of the sarge was even greater than her fear of Harold York. The sarge had been less diplomatic with her than I had been, and given her a proper roasting about withholding vital information about a suspect. He had not ruled out charging her.

We took Dottie to another room where half a dozen men were lined up, all dressed in trousers, shirts and a waistcoat. In those days there were no two-way mirrors. The accusers had to look the accused in the eye, and it was a terrifying experience for those who had to take part. A particularly aggressive-looking suspect could terrify a victim into silence.

I recognised a couple of them as fellow police officers from another station. Then there was Alf in his Sunday best, and another couple of men we often arrested for being drunk. They were paid a few bob for being in the line-up, so no doubt we would be arresting them again later that evening.

'Take your time,' the sarge told Dottie. 'And if you're not sure, it's all right to say so.'

'It's him,' she said immediately, pointing to the man on the number three spot. 'Number three. That's Harold York.'

'There's been some mistake,' the man she identified said. 'I've no idea who this York fellow is.'

'Take her out, Blandford. Then bring the next person in.'

'Well done,' I said to Dottie. 'You were very brave.' I bit my tongue to prevent me from saying that it was a pity she had not been as brave a few months earlier.

Nowadays I would be more understanding, but when one is young, you often fail to see things from the other side. Everything is black and white. My mother had understood Dottie's fears, perhaps because they were the same age and in the same situation, but I did not and would not for a very long time.

I saw Dottie back to her room, then went into the next room. 'Mr Rodgers?' I said with a welcoming smile. 'Please come through.'

He still had some bruising on his head, and he would always have the burns; but despite that, he looked well.

'The sarge thought it best to pretend I'd gone,' he had explained to me earlier. 'Element of surprise and all that.'

I almost hugged him, but thought better of it. 'I'm glad you're okay,' I said. 'Joe will be delighted.'

'He's a good lad. Shall we get this over with, lass?'

I nodded and led him into the line-up room. I heard an audible gasp when he entered the room but did not see where it came from.

Unlike Dottie Riley, Mr Rodgers took his time. He walked up and down the row of men, looking each in the face. 'Well that's Alf,' he said when he reached PC Norris. 'He's a copper.'

Alf rolled his eyes, but stayed in the line-up, whilst Rodgers took another turn.

'I knew who it was from the beginning,' he said, stopping in front of number three. 'I just wanted to be sure. I saw him in the pub, lording it up, and I knew straight away who he was. This is him. This is Harold York.'

'Thank you, Mr Rodgers,' said the sarge. He asked one of the other officers to take Mr Rodgers out. 'Give him a cup of tea and then take his statement,' he ordered. 'Go on, Blandford,' he said to me. 'This is your collar.'

'Really, Sarge?'

'Really. Get on with it.'

'I'm telling you there has been some mistake,' said number three.

'There's no mistake,' I said, walking up to the pub landlord, Brian Lancaster. 'Henry Brown, you are under arrest for the murders of Violet Johnson, Ruth Yates, Betty Norris and Harriet Johnson, and for the assault of Mr Norman Rodgers.'

* * *

'Would you like to explain it all, Blandford?' the sarge asked several days later when we were in his office. Alf Norris was with us, as were my mother, Dottie, Mrs Higgins and Mr Rodgers. Lancaster/Brown had been taken away kicking and screaming but had soon capitulated and admitted his guilt. He had written long letters to the chief constable, the home secretary and various newspapers, painting himself as a victim of circumstances, whilst not denying his crimes.

'I'll need more evidence from the Browns,' I said, 'to ensure he doesn't back down. I just hope she hasn't destroyed the photograph. I think she knew.'

'Who knew?' asked Mrs Higgins.

'Mrs Brown. I think she knew that her cousin had a violent streak. She probably told herself that the likes of Violet Johnson deserved it. She has told me some things since, but not every-thing. I've also been talking to people in

South America who knew him before he came to Britain. He was a wild child by all accounts, and always in trouble for stealing or fighting. When he was about sixteen he had tried to strangle a friend, insisting it was just a 'bit of fun'. No charges were brought against him. His family sent him to England to try to sort him out and he lived with Mrs Brown for a while, before moving on elsewhere.

'Violet and Daphne — Mrs Brown's daughter — had fallen out as teenagers and I didn't know why to begin with. Mrs Brown admitted that it was over Henry. He is the father of both Steve Brown and Harriet Johnson. Later, just before the war, he was staying with Mrs Brown again when he and Violet resumed their romance without Daphne to interfere. Violet's mother didn't know they were seeing each other again, as he had told Violet to give her a different name and he made sure they weren't seen together. Poor Mrs Johnson was not very astute at the best of times, due to her own problems with drink.

'The name Harold York, which he found at the cemetery in Scarborough, probably led to the Wars of the Roses theme in his fake names, and he used that name to join the RAF. It's my guess that the Paisley scarf he killed Violet with belonged to her. They fell out over something — his womanising or his propensity to steal, even from friends. I don't know why, and he's not saying.'

'So why the other murders?' asked Mrs Higgins. 'Why my sister Ruth and Alf's cousin Betty?'

'He said in a letter he wrote to the home secretary that he wanted to make it look like there was a killing spree, to remove suspicion from himself. Poor Ruth and Betty were his cover for killing Violet, and Mrs Riley very nearly was. Maybe finding the Paisley scarf when he broke into Mr Rodgers's locker gave him the idea, but I'm only guessing at that. The war and attitudes to women who were seen as having loose morals ended up being even better covers, and as we know now, he escaped justice for over twenty years.'

'So why did he murder this Harriet Johnson?' my mother asked. 'You say she was his daughter?'

'Losing a parent at such a young age has a marked effect on a child,' I said, remembering my own father. I could see in my mother's eyes that she was remembering too. 'It can either make them or break them. It broke Harriet Johnson. She also inherited some of Henry's nature. She was a petty thief, and obsessed with money. I found out from Mrs Scattergood that one of the things that Harriet had stolen just before she left her job for good was a Paisley scarf, similar to the one that he used to kill her mother. I don't know how she found out about Henry Brown . . . Brian Lancaster . . . or where to find him, and I don't suppose we ever will, as she's not here to tell us. I would like to think she came here to confront him for the sake of justice. But I'm more of a mind that she came here to blackmail him. After all, he was a businessman, and she probably thought he had money.'

'The bank was just about to default on the mortgage for the pub,' said the sarge. 'He hadn't been paying it and he'd used false information when applying for the loan.'

'That figures. So Harriet came to see him to cash in on his guilt, and he murdered her.' I shivered. 'It's chilling to think she brought the means of her own death. And you know the rest. Mr Rodgers, who hadn't been out of the house for years, went to the pub and saw the man he knew as Harold York.'

'I couldn't believe it,' said Mr Rodgers. 'He was older and fatter, so I wasn't sure at first. That's why I didn't come straight to the police. I had to know for certain, so I went back towards the pub. It was closed, but then I heard someone behind me. I said to him, 'I know it's you, Harold. I don't want any trouble.' Then he attacked me from behind. I don't remember much after that, but I suppose he must have moved me.'

The sarge nodded. 'Yes, that's right. We found you back at the crossroads.'

'Will I be charged?' asked Dottie Riley.

The sarge sighed. 'No, Dottie, you won't be charged. It wouldn't look very good if we prosecuted a victim, would it, now?'

I had not thought of Dottie as one of York's victims, but I realised then that she was. I still could not understand why she had hidden away for so long, letting him run loose, but I did have a little more sympathy for her.

Mrs Higgins had not said much, which was strange for her. 'Are you all right?' I asked her.

'I will be,' she said. I sensed that she wanted to say something to Dottie Riley, but some uncharacteristic tact stopped her. 'My sister wasn't a bad person, and I'm sure Betty Norris wasn't either. I think we should do something for them.

A memorial of some sort. What do you say, Alf?'

'Good idea, Martha. We'll ask the vicar, shall we?'

* * *

The memorial service took place just after Christmas. Life had been so hectic, with me helping to build up the case against Henry Brown, that I had barely seen Leo. I sensed he was avoiding me. I hadn't seen his wife either, and I had to learn from Mrs Higgins that she had gone back to America.

'Good riddance,' said Mrs Higgins as we drank tea and ate cake in her caravan. I had gone there to accompany her to the memorial service. 'You should have seen her swanning around the place whilst you were in Scarborough, acting like the lady of the manor.'

'Do you know when she's coming back?' I asked.

'I don't think she is. Hasn't Doctor Stanhope said anything to you?'

'We've hardly spoken for ages, except in passing. He probably thinks it's none of my business.'

'Then I don't know whose business it is,' said Mrs Higgins with a sniff. 'Men are so difficult. I told Laurence Olivier, either you sort it out with Jill Esmond or it's over. Then Vivien Leigh came along and snatched him from right under my nose.'

I could not help smiling. It showed that Mrs Higgins was back to her normal self.

'So, no more probation,' she said, smiling at me.

'Nope. I'm a full-fledged police officer now.'

'Will you be leaving us, Bobbie?' Mrs Higgins looked sad.

'I don't know, Mrs Higgins. The sarge says I can stay if I want, but I honestly don't know. Seeing Leo all the time . . . ' I paused, knowing she would understand the rest.

At five o'clock we walked arm in arm to the church. Snow had begun to fall, giving us an almost Dickensian setting that seemed to fit the mood.

Mrs Higgins had dressed especially in a bright purple pantsuit with a matching wide-brimmed hat. Compared to her usual garb it was quite subdued. I wore my uniform as, unbeknownst to Mrs Higgins, my colleagues and I from Stony End and other stations in the district had arranged to form a guard of honour as people left the church. It was as much for Alf as for Mrs Higgins, because we decided that Betty Norris, by dint of her relationship to him, had been one of us. As far as I was concerned, Mrs Higgins was one of us too.

We were at the town crossroads when I saw Leo walking down from the church towards us. 'May I talk to you for a moment, Bobbie? Please?'

'I have to get to the church,' I said.

'Go on,' said Mrs Higgins. 'Give the lad five minutes of your time. I won't let them start without us.'

He walked to the church with us, and then he and I carried on walking to the outskirts of town whilst Mrs Higgins went inside.

'I'm sorry I've kept away from you,' he said. 'I did have good reason.'

'Oh.'

'I didn't want to involve you in a scandal.'

'What scandal? You mean having an affair with you? I would have, you know. It's one of the reasons I came back from Scarborough.' It was the first time I had admitted that to myself, let alone to him.

'I know, but I wouldn't have let it happen.'

'Oh,' I said again.

'Not because I didn't want you, Bobbie. God knows how much I did. How much I still do. I don't care about my own reputation, but I wouldn't let you be sullied like that. You've seen what society thinks of women who make such mistakes. The papers have been rehashing it all about Ruth and Betty, even though their killer has proved to be a cold, hard man with no concerns other than for his own sorry hide. I won't let society do that to you.'

'So what do you want to tell me? Are you going to America to be with Cindy-Lou? Is that it?'

'There is no Cindy-Lou, Bobbie. There never was, as it turns out.'

I stopped and turned to face him. 'Now you're talking in riddles. Are you married or not?'

'Not. Never was. The man you saw when we got back from Scarborough . . .'

It had been a while so I had to rack my brains. 'Mr . . . Jones?'

'Johnson. He was a private investigator. I had him look into Cindy-Lou's background. It turned out that her real name was Gertrude Unwin, and I wasn't the only man she married that year in Las Vegas. I wasn't the first, either. She made a habit of it, and then touched them for money sometime down the line. She's been playing a long game. I sent her back to America on the understanding that I wouldn't press charges if she kept away from me and you. I've avoided you only because I didn't want you to be judged for taking up with me again so soon after a woman everyone thought was my wife had left.'

'So you're not married . . . '

'No.'

'But you thought you were. You were willing to give up everything for her.'

'No, I was willing to give up everything because I thought I had a son. I may be old-fashioned, but I think children need their parents.'

'Of course,' I said, shamefaced. 'What about your son? What about Mikey? Will she let you see him?'

'Mikey is five years old.'

'Yes, and . . . ?' I admit to being a bit slow on the uptake at the time, but I was still trying to come to terms with the fact that Leo was not married and never had been.

'Five years old, Bobbie. I was in Vegas ten years ago. Unless Cindy-Lou, alias Gertrude, had the gestation of an elephant — or two elephants — it doesn't add up.'

'Oh.' I imagine I was beginning to resemble a goldfish. 'Oh, Leo, I'm so sorry.'

'Thank you for that, my love. For understanding that it mattered to me. I admit to liking the idea of having a son, even if I didn't much like his mother. It was because she kept giving excuses as to why he couldn't come over that I got in touch with Mr Johnson to investigate.'

'That poor child though. He'd have been better off with you as a dad.'

'I like to think so. I did give her some money, to help him. Whether he'll see it or not is another matter.'

'Is there any chance that she could be pregnant now? She could turn up again in another ten years.'

'If she is, then I promise you it isn't my baby.'

'How can you be sure?'

He put his hands on my shoulders and drew me near. 'Do you really have to ask?'

'Hmm, that's just the sort of thing

men say. Or it's what the Italian said. That his wife hadn't let him touch her for years.'

'I didn't touch her. How could I? I was honest with her from the beginning that our marriage would be for Mikey's sake only. She tried to seduce me more than once. But I wasn't interested.'

I stood back, not sure I was ready to take the step of trusting him again, even though my heart was telling me to believe him. 'You kept a secret from me, Leo, for the second time since we've met. You broke my heart.' Hot tears filled my eyes. All the pain and anger I had tried so hard to suppress came flooding out. 'How many other secrets do you have? Other women? Children? A portrait in the attic, charting all your evil deeds?'

He smiled. 'I love you, Bobbie Blandford, and I know it's going to take you a while to trust me again, but I am going to earn that trust. No more secrets, I promise.' He held out his arms to me.

I hesitated. Then I put my hand in his, making it clear there would be no hugging just yet. I wiped my eyes with my other hand, my body a tumult of emotions — anger, relief, joy, love. They wrestled with each other, but eventually love won out. We walked down to the church, tentatively finding each other again. It could take a while, and it would not be an easy road for us, but I felt sure we would make it.

As we went down the aisle to take our place amongst our friends, he whispered, 'Promise me you won't run away again.'

What was the point of running away when my heart kept leading me back to Leo and to Stony End?

THE END

We do hope that you have enjoyed reading this large print book.

Did you know that all of our titles are available for purchase?

We publish a wide range of high quality large print books including:
Romances, Mysteries, Classics
General Fiction
Non Fiction and Westerns

Special interest titles available in large print are:
The Little Oxford Dictionary
Music Book, Song Book
Hymn Book, Service Book

Also available from us courtesy of Oxford University Press:
Young Readers' Dictionary
(large print edition)
Young Readers' Thesaurus
(large print edition)

For further information or a free brochure, please contact us at:
Ulverscroft Large Print Books Ltd.,
The Green, Bradgate Road, Anstey,
Leicester, LE7 7FU, England.
Tel: (00 44) 0116 236 4325
Fax: (00 44) 0116 234 0205